Praise for Joey Comeau's Overqualified

"There have been spoof letter-writing books in the past, like *The Lazlo Letters* by Don Novello (a.k.a. Father Guido Sarducci) and several that followed. While the protagonist in *Overqualified* is just as unhinged as his predecessors, he's significantly less giddy. A real story unfolds in these pages, about a departed brother and the sibling left behind. It's sad and fragmented and, in places, funny. This slender epistolary novel is charming." — *Los Angeles Times*

"[A] collection of wry, clever and demoniacal job-application letters, teeming with knife-edged malice and stomach-tearing hilarity. . . . *Overqualified* successfully deludes the fear of the faceless corporate entity by empowering the faceless applicant who has nothing to lose except securing a job he or she probably doesn't want. If Comeau's rebel-yell manifesto catches on like old Prometheus's gift did all those years ago, human resources will never be the same again." — *Globe and Mail*

"Joey Comeau's collection of real cover letters, *Overqualified* (ECW Press) is pretty much sui generis. Not to mention sweetly written, bitter and bitterly funny. . . . One of the season's most remarkable books." — *Macleans.ca*

"The letters are by turns hilarious and tragic, highly inappropriate and oversharing. The novel that results is both extremely funny and extremely sad, and above all, original — I've never read anything like it, and I want to read it again and again. . . . [Comeau] is a preternaturally skilled novelist, and he's written one of the most original and most affecting books I've read in years." — *Bookslut*

"Joey Comeau's *Overqualified* is Robert Silverberg's *Dying Inside* as redone by Steve Aylett. It's Don Novello's *The Lazlo Letters* as reinterpreted by Stanislaw Lem. It's Judy Blume's *Are you There God? It's me, Margaret* as chewed up and spit out by J. G. Ballard. This epistolary fantasia viscerally captures the insanity of capitalism and the marketplace and blends it with domestic and personal anguish to produce a book whose melancholy is leavened by a surprising hilarity. These are the awesomely goofy files of some alien or celestial Human Resources Department, delivered straight to your door as if by the Smoking Gun website." l Di Filippo,
aut l *Cosmocopia*

"If I were one of the lucky HR managers who received an Overqualified cover letter, I'm not sure I'd hire Joey Comeau. But I am sure that the next time I found myself lying awake in bed at 3 AM, I'd be reaching for his number." — Ryan North, *Dinosaur Comics*

"Each letter rapidly digresses into something more akin to a diary entry than a professional missive. There is speculation as to humanity's future, reminiscences from the narrator's childhood, confessions of vulnerability and of sexual desire, all punctuated by vitriolic humour and unsettling instances of violence. There is much frustration in these letters — born of capitalism's absurdities and of personal calamities — but there is also humour, compassion, and joy." — *Quill & Quire*

"*Overqualified* is unlike anything you've ever read. Each of Joey Comeau's letters comments, sometimes subtly, sometimes not, on the emptiness of the system to which we bow during a job search while it simultaneously reveals the humor, beauty, and pain that is all else in life, which, Joey Comeau wants you to realize, is short." — *About.com*

A sometimes-hilarious, sometimes-crushingly sad romp through a man's swelling nihilism and disenchantment. . . . This book is very much about nostalgia for a past of exaggerated quirks and curious beauty. So many of us are compelled to believe these things are on the fringes, are odd and unordinary, but this little novella, much like Miranda July of David Eggers' stories, tries to portray these things unashamedly, as 'something that feels perfect and correct.'" — *MonstersAndCritics.com*

"[*Overqualified*] has found a permanent home in my collection of books that have changed the way I look at and think about the world around me. . . . The book is chaotic and contradictory; incomplete, yet full of life; full of charm and wit and character." — *The Uniter*

"Joey Comeau's new novel *Overqualified* delivers an addictively humorous and dark alternative to the stone-cold task of getting employers to know you through a piece of paper. . . . *Overqualified* is a quick read, but crackles with hilarious desperation and deadpan sincerity. With these humorous letters, Comeau reveals how life is actually lived, and not just marketed." — *FFWD*

"I guarantee that you will laugh out-loud at least once and that you will try to share what was so funny with someone who will just stare at you like you are a freak." — *410Media.com*

"The sincerity with which he writes is mesmerizing, and even though each cover letter is a scant two pages, they're full of painful emotion. It's a unique way to tell a story and definitely worth checking out."
— *The Arizona Daily Wildcat*

"*Overqualified* is the type of book you don't read, you devour. Because the book is a series of letters, it's short, and you can read it at your leisure. Maybe you can finish it in an afternoon, but you'll never truly stop reading it. Years from now, you'll unbind your tattered first edition, flip through the pages and reread an especially meaningful letter."
— *Jack Central*

"*Overqualified* fears no depths. It is unpredictably humorous. It is intriguingly disgusting. It is profoundly sad. And it's sexy, in ways we might not admit out loud. The narrator's internal complexities make the usually sterile cover letter form pulse with breath and blood. . . . If you've ever felt crazy, this book will help you realize that you're not alone. If you've ever felt normal, this book will show you what you've been missing."
— *Austinist*

"[A] magnificent and timely curiosity . . . The letters are baffling and amusing at times, poignant or obsessive on other occasions. . . . During a time of economic uncertainty — when the practical and the existential seem eerily akin — *Overqualified* expresses the irrepressible humanity at the heart of our industries, and affirms the fruits of our many labours."
— *Scene Magazine*

"For anyone who has had the grievous task of summing up the core of their experience and extracting suitable parts of their personality to submit in a cover letter, author Joey Comeau's novel, *Overqualified*, is a breath of fresh air."
— *Buzzine*

"Ranging from pithy and heartwarming to darkly funny and bizarre, the letters sparkle with the inappropriate use of unabashed personal honesty in a traditionally dry and humourless form. . . . [*Overqualified* is] beautifully executed satire, perfect for anyone who needs a good laugh (like the unemployed)."
— *Geist*

one bloody thing after another

Joey Comeau

MISFIT

ECW Press

Published by ECW Press, 2120 Queen Street East, Suite 200,
Toronto, Ontario, Canada M4E 1E2 / 416.694.3348 / info@ecwpress.com

LIBRARY AND ARCHIVES CANADA CATALOGUING IN PUBLICATION

Comeau, Joey, 1980-
One bloody thing after another / Joey Comeau.

ISBN 978-1-55022-916-5

I. Title.

PS8605.O537O54 2010   C813'.6   C2009-905969-X

Editor for the press: Michael Holmes / a misFit book
Layout and design: Rachel Ironstone
Cover image: Emily Horne
Printing: Webcom   1   2   3   4   5

Mixed Sources
Product group from well-managed
forests, controlled sources and
recycled wood or fiber
www.fsc.org Cert no. SW-COC-002358
© 1996 Forest Stewardship Council

ANCIENT FOREST ™
FRIENDLY

The publication of *One Bloody Thing After Another* has been generously supported by
the Canada Council for the Arts, which last year invested $20.1 million in writing and
publishing throughout Canada, by the Ontario Arts Council, by the Government of
Ontario through Ontario Book Publishing Tax Credit, by the OMDC Book Fund, an
initiative of the Ontario Media Development Corporation, and by the Government of
Canada through the Book Publishing Industry Development Program (BPIDP).

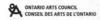

printed and bound in CANADA

For Maggie and for Hamilton

prologue

Ann's mother isn't feeling so good today

The window in the upstairs hallway is open. No wonder it was so cold last night. Ann slides it closed, hard, and goes down to the kitchen. There's a bowl of cereal laid out for her breakfast, and Ann's younger sister Margaret is already shoveling food into her face. Milk dribbles down Margaret's chin. There's cereal all over the tabletop.

"You're disgusting," Ann says. "Your friends will wait for you, you know. You don't have to choke it down like that."

"Hey, go slow," their mother says, coming into the kitchen. She's dressed up, in a gray-and-white suit, and she twirls once for her daughters. "What do you think?" she says. "Professional? Hire-able? Is the red scarf too much?"

"You look great, Mom," Ann tells her. Margaret just keeps eating. Their mother bends down to get something from the floor. It's a couple seconds before Ann realizes that her mother hasn't come up again. She leans over, and sees that her mom wasn't picking something up at all. She's crouched down, holding a hand to her throat.

"Are you okay?" Ann says.

"Yeah. Yeah, I'm fine, Ann." Her mother clears her throat. "Sorry. I just have something. . . ." she clears her throat again louder, and then stands up, smiling. She clears her throat again. Then again.

Even Margaret is looking up from her cereal. Their mother coughs. And then she coughs harder. There's a bit of blood on her lips now.

She smiles.

"Wish me luck today!" she says.

II

Ann's mother was perfectly qualified, but her interview did not go well. Afterward, she ran out of the conference room holding her red scarf over her mouth, leaving two men, Jeff and Alex, sitting in silence for a long time.

Between the two of them they have interviewed thousands of men and women for various jobs. It has never before gone so ridiculously badly. They're just sitting there. They should clean this up and call the next applicant. They're on a schedule, after all. But instead they sit in silence.

Alex looks at the door where she ran out, and then he looks at the wet, bloody chunk of god-knows-what sitting on the table in front of them. The thing she coughed up, partway through the interview. That poor woman.

"That did not go well," Jeff says.

He can joke because none of the blood landed on him.

One Bloody Thing After Another

part 1

What do I do without you?

Tell

1

Charlie worries sometimes that his dog is an idiot. When Mitchie wants to lie down, he just falls over on his side. When he gets excited, he pees a little. But what can Charlie do? You can't take a dog back after fifteen years and say, "You gave me a lemon." Charlie's too old to find another dog, anyway.

At the end of his leash, Mitchie is laid out on his side in the middle of the crosswalk, panting. In a minute these cars are going to start honking, but right now the drivers are probably struck dumb at the sight of a dog this stupid.

"God damn it, Mitchie," Charlie says. "Come on."

her

There are tree branches on the ground in the backyard. They're not attached to the tree, like branches ought to be. They're severed. Sawed off. This was Jackie's first-kiss tree, and it used to hang over the backyard, back when this was Jackie's yard. Back when 10 Osborne Street was her address and the curtains were blue.

Two blocks down that way is her broken-arm tree. She has a car-accident tree, too. There is a tree at the hospital where Jackie's mother passed away into the long goodnight. And when Jackie gets lonely, or sad, she goes and she finds one of her trees.

Her first kiss was with a boy named Carl when she was ten years old. Carl told everyone at school that they'd made out. He said she kissed him and that he put his hand up her shirt. For one week Jackie was the great big slut of grade 5.

But she didn't kiss him. He kissed her. And in return he got kicked in the shin. At the time it didn't even seem important. It was just one more stupid thing she was supposed to like but didn't. Jackie doesn't even really remember the kiss.

She remembers how Carl's mother came to pick him up that day, and that dog jumped out of the back of the car and ran right at Jackie, smelling like the woods and like fire and like the ocean, all at the same time.

But it was her first kiss, and the first sign of her indifference to boys. She'd been indifferent before then, of course. But indifference is hard to notice until you're in a situation where you're supposed to care.

Jackie visits her trees and she remembers. Or sometimes she doesn't remember. It helps just to sit under them. It's familiar. And her trees are always okay. They have a nice little visit together and Jackie goes home.

But today is different. Today there are branches everywhere, bright wood exposed. Her tree is cut down. And Jackie bites the inside of her cheek to keep calm.

She knocks on the front door of the house, all gentle and polite like a lady. Like a gentlewoman. She knocks again. The door has a knocker, below the big Welcome sign. Jackie makes herself smile, in case she looks as angry as she feels. Her father always says, "Anger never solves anything."

Mrs. Hubert answers the door.

"Pardon me, ma'am," Jackie says.

"Oh hello, dear." Mrs. Hubert is in a housecoat. Jackie is wearing her Sunday best.

"Pardon me, ma'am. I'm sorry to interrupt your Sunday, but I just wondered if I could ask you a question. What happened to that big, old tree in your backyard?" Jackie says. And Jackie smiles. She is all sweetness, prim and proper.

"Oh, we needed some light back there," Mrs. Hubert says, smiling back at her. "Jim bought a barbeque, but it's always so dark. We thought, wouldn't it be nicer for the grandkids if there were some sunlight back there in the afternoon? My son came out this morning with his chainsaw. It really opens up the backyard, don't you think?"

"Oh, it certainly does." Jackie is chewing the inside of her cheek. She keeps thinking, *anger doesn't solve anything,* but she can taste blood.

"Are . . . are you bleeding?" Mrs. Hubert says. "Your lips!"

And then, violence. Jackie picks up the biggest rock she can find, and she carries it to the driveway. She puts it right through the window of Mrs. Hubert's car. *Smash.* It feels good. She loves that sound exactly because it makes no sense. There's broken glass on the pavement and everywhere. It's on the car seats and on Jackie's dark sneakers. All her arm hair is standing up. Her muscles are warm. Her mouth tastes like blood.

Mrs. Hubert, of 10 Osborne Street, won't be calling her *dear* again anytime soon. Jackie's Sunday best gave the old woman an incorrect first impression. Mrs. Hubert saw a young girl, clean and well dressed, fancy black pants and a nice white shirt, and she thought it was one of the proper young ladies from her church. It wasn't. It was one of those proper young ladies she sees being helped into police cruisers on the TV news at night.

So now Mrs. Hubert has her front door locked, to keep Jackie out. It's a heavy wooden door, with a sign in the center that has the word *Welcome* burned into it. The curtains look like lace in the small half circle window at the top. This would be easier if Mrs. Hubert didn't look so scared. She's yelling something that Jackie can't hear. Police, police, police. Something like that. She has a phone in her hand.

Jackie looks like the bad guy here. Mrs. Hubert is crying and Jackie is all covered with violence and broken glass. But Jackie isn't the bad guy. The tree was cut down. Jackie's first-kiss tree. And so Jackie is angry. But she didn't start smashing things right away. She went over to the house. She rang the doorbell. She was a nice young lady with some questions about that old tree in the backyard.

"Pardon me, ma'am," Jackie had said.

"Oh hello, dear," Mrs. Hubert said.

Jackie is just as surprised as anybody. She didn't come out here to break windows. She came out here to visit her tree. When she got off the bus, there was no blood in her mouth at all. She was quiet, thinking about her friend Ann. Visiting her trees always helps Jackie think. But now her thoughts are thinking themselves for her. Her body knows what to do. She lifts up the second big rock. She's confused by how heavy it is. She almost can't handle it. It's been a long time since she lifted anything this heavy.

She aches. She stumbles a bit. How many trees get cut down every day? What if every one of those trees had someone who cared? Someone to avenge it? Jackie is just a good girl, doing her part for the environment. *Smash!*

Now there are two big rocks in the shiny, gray car. She leans her head in through the window of Mrs. Hubert's car and brushes the glass off the passenger seat rock. She pulls the seat belt across and fastens it securely. She tugs to make sure it doesn't come undone.

The rock looks so handsome with the black seat belt around it. So does the first rock. This is nice. It paints a pretty picture. Out for a Sunday drive with the windows down.

Mister and Missus Rock.

Lovely.

"I'm calling the police!" yells Mrs. Hubert from inside. She has the window open a crack. She doesn't sound angry; she should sound angry, she should get righteous about her car windows. She's supposed to be the bad guy, not the victim. But she has her lines all wrong. She sounds scared. "Please stop," she says.

And Jackie's not a monster. She hears the fear in Mrs. Hubert's voice and suddenly she can see what this looks like from the other side.

Mrs. Hubert cut down a tree. Everyone cuts down trees.

She didn't even do it herself. This was just a bit of yard work, one of a dozen chores her son helps her with. She called him and he came out in the morning with a coffee in one hand and a chainsaw in his trunk and he cut down a tree and poor Mrs. Hubert had no way of knowing about Jackie's first kiss underneath that tree.

She had no way of knowing that Jackie had spent all last night going over and over in her head what she would say to Ann. It is not an easy thing for a girl to ask her best friend on a date. Oh god.

But Mrs. Hubert couldn't have known any of this.

The tree is in pieces on the ground. Cut down. Jackie needed to see it today. She needed to sit underneath it, but she can't. When Jackie saw Ann at school today, down at the other end of the hallway, she waved. She waved and Ann closed her locker and walked away, like she didn't see. Maybe she didn't see.

It was just a chore to Mrs. Hubert. It was a bit of yard work, and then she answered her door and said, "Oh hello, dear," and then violence. Jackie knows that Mrs. Hubert isn't the bad guy.

But what can Jackie do? Run? There's already glass everywhere, and if she doesn't look over and see Mrs. Hubert's face, this feels right. On this side of the door there are no tear-stained faces. Just tree branches on the ground, and justice. Jackie shakes her head. No. It isn't right. She should stop. She should leave Mrs. Hubert alone and just run. This isn't right.

She bends down and picks up another big rock.

You know how mothers play Mozart against their bellies during pregnancy? Jackie's mother went around swinging a tire iron, bashing headlights in the street all night, belly enormous. Who else could say their mother had been in a riot while pregnant? Kicking in windows while little Jackie grew inside.

Throwing bottles against police cars while little Jackie listened and learned. That was the real Patricia. She was the glass-bashing mayhem, even pregnant. Good old Tire Iron Pat. She wouldn't be caught dead in a hospital gown. Or crying. Well, Jackie is her mother's daughter. *Smash!*

The glass sounds so perfect.

Anger seems to be solving this quite nicely, actually. Her father never got angry about anything. Sometimes he took his glasses off, and he folded and unfolded them really slowly, but he never got angry. He wrote letters to his local representative, instead.

"That's how you get things done, chickadee," he said. He calls his daughter chickadee now that they live together. He didn't have a nickname for her before, when her mother was still alive.

Mrs. Hubert opens the window further. "I'm calling the police!" she yells. Jackie can hear the fear in Mrs. Hubert's voice, but she yells right back at her anyway.

"It's really opening up the back seat, don't you think?" Jackie says.

3

"It is an ordeal," Charlie tells his dog. "Walking you is an ordeal."

Mitchie isn't listening. He's licking the filthy hands of apparently homeless children. Again. Every day with this. His stump of a tail is wagging like crazy.

"Don't you go to school? Don't you have mothers?" Charlie says to the children. But they don't answer him. The blond one with the missing teeth looks like he might have several mothers. Mitchie loves the attention, though, and so Charlie tolerates them a while longer. The things he will go through for that dog.

When the children are gone, Mitchie looks up at Charlie with cloudy eyes. Cataracts make the little guy half blind, but he doesn't seem to care. It hasn't changed him at all. There's a siren nearby, getting louder. Truant officers, probably.

I'm

4

Jackie can hear the siren, not too far away. She reaches into the back seat of the car and brushes the glass off the little boy rock. She kicks glass off her sneaker. The cuff of her pants is full of glass.

All the car's windows are broken and she doesn't feel any better. This was a mistake. She could run. She knows these backyards. She grew up here. She could be long gone before the police arrive. But nothing feels right.

The sirens are getting louder, and she's having trouble thinking new thoughts. She is supposed to leave before the police arrive, but they're early. They cut the siren. The police cruiser pulls into the driveway, slow and calm. They're so quiet now.

They are getting out of the car, and Jackie's all covered in glass. Mrs. Hubert comes outside, and she's crying.

"I didn't know what to do," Mrs. Hubert says. "I didn't want to call, but I was so scared. And then I was worried she would hurt herself."

Jackie wants to touch her. Or calm her down somehow. But if she does, she knows that she'll start crying too. She has to stay strong. She is her mother's daughter. Jackie looks away from the older woman and grinds the glass under her shoe. *Focus.* What is Jackie supposed to say?

She could try to explain about her tree. About all the trees, and about memories. But that's not all this was. This was some kind of tantrum, too. And it will feel worse to pretend it wasn't. Better not to explain at all. One of the cops pulls out his handcuffs.

"That's embarrassing," Jackie says to him. "You both wore the same outfit today."

"Two grown men with guns for one dumb kid. Do you see that, Mitchie?" Charlie reaches down to untangle Mitchie's leash from where the fat little idiot has wrapped it around the bus stop. Mitchie, meanwhile, is busy wrapping himself around Charlie's leg. "You want me to fall over right here on the sidewalk, is that it?" Charlie says to his dog. Mitchie looks up at him happily.

"Come on, Mitchie," Charlie says, and they start up the hill again. It's none of their business what goes on in people's driveways. It is not their problem. Charlie loops the leash around his hand. At the next pole, Mitchie stops to do his business. Then Charlie starts pulling Mitchie up the road again. They stop at the next pole, too. A little girl in a pink dress comes down the driveway from her house.

Will it never end?

"Have you seen Wednesday?" she says. She's holding out a poster with a crude drawing of a cat on it. Charlie doesn't even pretend to look at the picture.

"No," he says.

The little girl holds out the poster again. "My cat Wednesday ran away," she says. Mitchie's fat little tail is going berserk now that he's heard the little girl's voice. She bends down to pet him, and he starts licking her like they're old friends. She says, "Oh, hello! How about you? Have you seen Wednesday?"

What is she, slow?

"No he hasn't," Charlie says. "He's been with me all day."

"She's real small, and she's all black except for her nose," the little girl says to Mitchie.

"We have to go." Charlie pulls on the leash and waves her off with his other hand. She stands watching as Mitchie and Charlie start walking up the hill again.

Mitchie stops at the next lamppost. Charlie looks back at the little girl, making sure she doesn't take this as a sign to start talking to them again.

"Christ almighty, Mitchie. I want to get home. How would you like it if we stopped at every house, so I could go inside and use their toilet?"

Mitchie doesn't care — he'd probably like that just fine.

The cop says "Sorry" when he cuffs Jackie's hands behind her back. He guides her head gently as he helps her into the cruiser. Jackie doesn't fight. Then both cops go to talk to Mrs. Hubert, and Jackie is stuck listening to the police radio with her hands cuffed under her butt.

It's uncomfortable sitting on handcuffs. Jackie rolls over on her left leg, which isn't comfortable, either. She rolls over on her right leg. The police radio people are having a great time, using their code words and sounding very official. "One-Mike-one, are you dealing with a fifty-one-fifty?" Jackie can hear her own breathing too clearly. The first-kiss tree used to be between the house and that fence. You could have seen it from here. It's gone.

Maybe if she had come yesterday she could have saved her tree. But that's stupid. If she came yesterday it would have been there and she would have sat underneath and thought about Carl and his rat-tail haircut and his dog. Then, the next time she got sad, she would have come and found nothing. She would have rung the doorbell then. This would have happened either way.

After a few minutes, the cops close their notebooks and Mrs. Hubert comes over to the car with them. The cops stand and talk some more, ignoring Jackie for now, but Mrs. Hubert looks down through the window. Jackie smiles at her before she even realizes what she's doing. Mrs. Hubert looks startled.

And then the cops are in the car and they're driving. Jackie feels a bit better now. Mrs. Hubert is okay. She probably has insurance. It was just glass. And now Jackie feels strong and tough, handcuffed in the back of the police car, driving through her old neighborhood. She couldn't protect her tree, but at least she *did* something.

The cops keep trying to get her name. Jackie just looks out the window. There go the tennis courts. When she was in elementary school, she used to come down through the path in those woods every day to play basketball. There's a path through the backyards of these houses, a shortcut to and from school. Trees and rocks and little Jackie's backpack and juice containers. She doesn't remember if she felt strong and tough back then.

The cruiser stops behind a bus, and a bunch of girls get out. They're younger than Jackie and they've all got matching school jackets. Two of them look over, and Jackie wishes she could wave. The girls are all watching now, hoping to recognize her from school. Jackie always used to get excited when she saw a police car with someone in the back. Was it a murderer? A shoplifter? Murderers probably wish they could wave, too.

The cop car turns right, at the corner where you turn left to get to the broken-arm tree.

At the police station, the cops put Jackie in a room with a big mirror along one wall like a blackboard. They tell her that they're going to call someone from youth services. She's not really listening. She still hasn't told them her name.

"I'm not stupid," she says. "I watch TV."

The cop writes something down on his piece of paper.

"Go soak your head," Jackie tells him.

Someone has carved initials into the table. *P.H.* There's a line under it. Those are the same as her mother's initials. Maybe they *are* her mother's initials. Could be. Jackie wonders how old this table is. The wood is stained a dark colour and it's oily looking. *Tire Iron Pat*, she thinks, and she smiles.

The cop smiles back. "Did you carve that?" he says.

"You know I didn't carve it. You were watching from the other side of the mirror." She touches the *P.H.* with her fingertip. It's smooth. Old.

"We don't have to be enemies," the cop says. "I'd love to get your side of the story. That's all."

Jackie rolls her eyes. "There is nothing you can say to a cop that will ever help you," she says.

Her mother taught her that.

okay.

Every day, in the front lobby of the retirement home, Mitchie gets stuck in the corner. He gets too excited, coming back from his walk, pulling at his leash. And every day Charlie has to help him.

"Careful, Mitchie. Watch where you're going." But poor blind Mitchie hobbles into that corner anyway. He's reliable. Every day, stuck in the corner. And every day, without fail, that woman is standing on the other side of the glass door, her own severed head in her arms, watching them.

Charlie opens the door, and he gives Mitchie's leash a sharp tug. The fat little dog pulls back a bit, and then walks into the wall again. He totters from foot to foot. The headless woman is still standing there, blocking the way, blood trickling. She's talking, and Charlie can see her lips moving, but no sound is coming out. If he was a younger man, maybe he could read her lips a bit, but his eyesight isn't so good anymore. Charlie is getting tired of her anyway. He pulls at the leash again.

"God damn it, Mitchie," Charlie says. "Come on, now."

Mitchie has himself turned around the right way, and he starts toward Charlie, panting a bit. Each little step is an effort. He walks right past the door again, and Charlie has to give the leash another tug, to turn him in the right direction. They squeeze past the woman, and Charlie grits his teeth against the cold where he brushes against her skin. He can feel her eyes looking up at him.

"What do you think she wants today, Mitch?" Charlie asks the dog. They're in the elevator lobby now. "She just won't give it up, eh? What was it yesterday?" Charlie turns to the ghost. She's on the other side of the lobby. "Is it your email again? Are you having trouble with your email?"

The ghost takes a shaking step toward them. She's off balance, not that Charlie could blame her. Having your head cut off would certainly affect your equilibrium. She takes another step, and then another. She's so slow. Mitchie is chewing on himself while they wait.

Margaret and Ann are home from school. Downstairs their mother is waking up again. They can hear her voice through the basement door. No words yet, just a constant howling. An animal sound. It will get worse as the night goes on.

"This is stupid. We know what she needs," Margaret says, putting her books on the table. Ann shakes her head again.

"No," she says.

"Don't be an idiot," Margaret says. "The hamster and the bird were both alive. That's the connection, and that's what she needs."

Ann knows her sister is right. But they have to be sure. Of course they have to be sure. Why is this so easy for Margaret? Already it's "the hamster and the bird," and not Herman and Blue Guy.

"We have to try other things," Ann says. "What about raw meat? We can get something fresh from the grocery store. The best steak they have. Or we could try fish. Or dog food."

"We're not feeding her dog food," Margaret says. "Jesus. She's our mother."

Tell

"We want you to call your parents." A new cop takes Jackie to a small room with lots of old desks and bored-looking police officers. They have old computers too, and old telephones, and everyone is frowning.

"Good evening, everybody!" Jackie says. Her head is clear now. That tree is dead and gone. Okay. That is not what she would have chosen, but it's done now and she is in a new situation and she has to act accordingly. Ann ignored her at school, but that is not the problem on the table at this time. Ann didn't know Jackie was going to ask her out. She couldn't have known. It wasn't a rejection because Jackie didn't get a chance to even ask.

Clear your head, Jackie thinks. It is not time to worry. It is time to escape.

The police are still frowning.

"Are you this unhappy all the time?" Jackie says. But they don't look unhappy. They look bored. She wishes she had a water balloon. That would cheer them up. *Splash!* Why do they keep coming to their jobs if they hate it here so much? She wants to tell them that they can escape with her when she goes.

"Press nine to call out," bored cop #1 says. He is all business, Jackie thinks, and these people are in the business of frowning. Well, not Jackie. Jackie is in the business of escape. Jackie is in the business of magic, and magicians always tell jokes.

She picks up the phone and presses nine for an outside line, just like the cop says. Nothing up my sleeve! Can we all agree that this is just a regular telephone, ladies and gentlemen? But she doesn't dial her own telephone number. Her father wouldn't be home anyway. Jackie dials the number for the police station, which is printed right on the phone itself. Line two starts flashing. The phone on the next desk begins to ring.

"Yes?" bored cop #2 says into her phone.

"Is your refrigerator running?" Jackie says.

11

Ann looks down at her homework but still can't seem to see it. All day she went to classes. Wrote down notes. Anything to try to forget about what was happening. She didn't even see Jackie. What would she have said? But now she regrets it. She should have gone and found her. Not to tell her. Just to see her. Tomorrow she'd go and find her friend.

Downstairs Ann's mother is screaming the same word over and over again, "Taste, taste, taste, taste, taste!" and Ann can hear Margaret's quiet voice, trying to soothe her.

The plate breaks against the wall down there, and then silence. Ann looks down at the homework and she wants to believe that their mother is eating the steak they bought her. The silence goes on and on and after a while it gets easier for Ann to believe this. She should be down there, too. She shouldn't have made her sister do this alone.

She hears Margaret again, singing a song that Ann forgot they even knew. It's been so long. It was a song they only ever heard when they went camping.

Ann remembers the cabin by the lake. Their mother carrying Margaret screaming out into deeper water, shampoo in Margaret's hair. The terrible blackness of the outhouse at night. Frogs on the wooden step. The way the lake shone first thing in the morning.

And every night, sitting in the dark with the wood stove giving the room just the smallest bit of light, their mother would sing to them. Ann hasn't heard that song in years. She'd forgotten it.

Margaret is downstairs, singing it now, to calm their mother down.

But the screaming begins again. "Taste, taste, taste, taste, taste, taste, taste!" The word sounds wrong, because the shape of their mother's mouth has been changing.

12

They want to take her fingerprints. But Jackie knows how that works. They take her picture and her fingerprints and they put all that information about her inside a computer. Strangers will know things.

"Oh, we knew just where to find you because of computer science! You were on file and in our database so we caught you really easily."

No thank you, Jackie thinks. So she tells the cop that she has to go to the bathroom, and she uses her little girl voice. He waits right outside the door with his gun, so that Jackie can't escape, but she's going to escape anyway.

Inside the bathroom, Jackie climbs up on the gray counter beside the sink and sits with her back up against the corner. The paint on the walls here is a mustard yellow. Once, her mom told her that hospitals paint the walls yellow because it calms people down. Jackie pulls her knees to her chest and for a few seconds she feels stupid and scared. But there is no other way to escape. Outside that door there is only a computer waiting for the cops to put Jackie inside it. There are no windows in here.

She always forgets this part, how gross it feels, how hard it is to make herself do it. All she can think about now is how awful it will be. But there are no windows in here. They thought of that. Maybe there used to be windows, but too many people escaped. The yellow paint didn't calm them down enough. This is a police station, and there is only one way out. Jackie hugs her legs tighter, and she feels a bit sick. Outside, the cop knocks.

"Come on," he says. "Hurry up."

This is her own fault. She should have run away when the cops pulled up to the house instead of just telling stupid jokes. Now she has no choice. The inside of her face tastes like blood again. The cop pounds on the door again, and turns the knob. The door starts to swing inward.

"Mom," Jackie says, under her breath. This is her magic word.

She is a computer shutting down. Her senses all go quiet like programs closing one by one. This part is fine. This is the good part. She can't hear the buzz of the lights anymore. The room isn't hot anymore. Jackie is not really there. She's in a secret place, and from that secret place she can see the cop step into the bathroom, but can't hear what he is saying. He looks behind the bathroom door, then closes it. He says something else. She can see his lips moving. He looks around. He looks right through her.

Jackie doesn't really know where she is. She's on the counter, but she's not on the counter. This is like TV. Her father works in TV, and at the studio they have a big room that is a bedroom and a kitchen and a living room and a basement with a pool table all lined up. People stand in one part and pretend there are walls, and on camera it looks separate. But it isn't really. Jackie is sitting right on the couch, but the cameras are all pointed at the dining room table. Nobody can see her.

The cop is pushing open the doors to the stalls, one by one. She's not behind the doors, though. She's behind the camera. She's invisible.

He kneels down and looks for her sneakers under the stall. Then he opens the door. Door number one, no Jackie. Door number two, no Jackie. There's only one more door. Jackie can hear the scratching already. Her mother's breathing sounds like scratching. It's the only thing Jackie can hear in the whole bathroom.

The floor is shiny. Under the door Jackie sees wet blue light. When the cop opens the stall door, it floods into the room. He doesn't see anything. He says something Jackie can't hear into his radio and he runs out.

Jackie can see her, though. It is her mother's ghost, in a stained hospital gown, kneeling in front of the toilet, waiting for more vomit to come, head down. Her shoulders jerk up, and she makes a sound in her throat, but she doesn't vomit.

"Jackie," she says, "go to bed." The ghost dry heaves. Then dry heaves again. She will vomit, though. She'll be up all night. There is always more vomit.

"Jackie, I am okay."

The bathroom tiles look cold in the blue light. Jackie can step outside of things, some kind of magic that makes her invisible, but it's never easy. It isn't like waving a wand. It costs.

"I didn't mean to wake you, baby." Somewhere the police run around the building trying to find Jackie. She's escaped! They don't know how, but she's escaped. Jackie sits down on the floor next to her mother, and she rubs the ghost's back through the gown. Her mother doesn't look up from the toilet. She squeezes the rim with her fingers. "Go back to sleep, Jackie," she says. "I'm okay."

her

13

Jackie's father is still at work when she gets home. Her mouth tastes like hospitals. Jackie has a map in her room, showing all of her trees. It's huge on the wall. There is a green pin for each tree. She pulls the pin out of Number 10 Osborne Street. There is no tree there now. The first-kiss tree. Goodbye Carl. Goodbye Carl's mom and Carl's dog. She puts the pin back in the box where it came from and she picks out a black one. It is the first black pin on the map.

Tomorrow will be different. Jackie won't let her worries overwhelm her. She knows what to say to Ann. And this time she'll say it: "Would you like to go on a date with me?"

Jackie puts the box of pins back in the drawer, and sits on her bed. She pushes the pillow aside and lies flat on her back.

Maybe she could tell Ann about her mother's ghost. Jackie hasn't told anyone. She hasn't wanted to tell anyone. But maybe it would help Ann understand her. Help them get closer. Probably, though, it would just freak her out.

Outside the window, the leaves are moving a bit in the wind. No. Keep it simple: "Will you go out on a date with me, Ann?"

This is their daily ritual. The ghost leads Charlie and Mitchie down the long hallway. The hallways on this floor are more quaint than the ones upstairs. There's a potted plant on the table there. The tablecloth is cream-colored lace. The ghost stops in front of Mrs. Richards' door and waits. Room 135. Every day. Charlie knocks. The door opens, and here comes Mrs. Richards, laundry basket in hand.

"Charles," Mrs. Richards says, "that dog of yours was barking again last night."

The ghost is staring up at her, its face expressionless. It lifts its head under one arm, and raises its other hand to point. Now, what does that mean? Every day. Knock on Mrs. Richards' door, and then what? The ghost just stands there, pointing, drooling black blood on the carpet. Charlie wants to help her, but he has no idea how. What does she want?

And Mrs. Richards is always accusing Mitchie of barking, even though it's been years since he's been able to make a sound. Charlie doesn't mind, though. She's not so bad. Some people just like to complain. At least she's got some spark left in her, not like the other people in this place. No, Mrs. Richards is fine. Let her complain about Mitchie. It doesn't faze Mitchie, so why should Charlie care?

The ghost is a different story. The ghost won't leave him alone. Does she want him to tell Mrs. Richards something? Does she have some spooky missive from beyond the grave?

"Do you know anyone who got their head cut off, Mrs. Richards?"

"If you don't keep him quiet, I'll have to make a formal complaint, Charles," she says. "Honestly. The dog barks all night, and then you come knocking on my door. Oh hello Charles. How are you today? Can I help you? Oh, you just want to talk more about a headless ghost that follows you and that stupid dog of yours around? I guess I'll see you tomorrow. Well, you know what, Charles? I would prefer if I didn't see you tomorrow. Knock on somebody else's door tomorrow with your idiot dog."

"My dog is not an idiot," Charlie says. But when he looks down Mitchie is standing with his face pressed against the wall again. "Turn around and defend yourself, Mitchie, for the love of Christ."

The ghost is still pointing a bloody finger in Mrs. Richards' face. Its lips are sounding out empty words. What does it want? Who has time for this nonsense?

Every stupid day.

15

The wood under Jackie's feet is slippery. She moves forward, trying to get a better grip with her sneakers, but that isn't going to be enough. She needs to reach out a free hand and steady herself, except Ann would think less of her. Ann has her black hair clipped up. Even in the pouring rain it looks good.

"You can give up, if you'd like," Jackie says. "There's only a little shame in defeat." Their hands are lashed together with a bandana. This is a fight to the death, Jackie thinks. They are standing on top of this playground equipment in the rain like they don't have the sense they were born with. The broken-arm tree is wide above them, but Ann doesn't know that. She thinks this is just a straightforward fight to the death, without symbolism. Jackie's foot slides again. Don't look down, she thinks. But looking at Ann makes her dizzy, too.

"Give up," she says again.

"No," Ann tells her.

"I'm just saying," Jackie says, "it'll probably hurt less. Have you noticed how high up we are?" But Ann isn't scared. "If you give up now," Jackie says, "nobody needs to know you were scared. We can tell people you had *female problems*."

It wasn't raining when they'd got on the streetcar to come out here, but it sure is raining now. They'd climbed up the hill to the playground anyway.

Jackie fell out of that tree up there, years ago, when there was no playground equipment here. She was hanging upside down, with her arms and hair reaching for the ground. She had long hair, then. She had skinny arms. But she didn't have much in the way of common sense.

She was up there, flipping around on the branch like Jackie the little gymnast, way up in a tree with no one around. She could have snapped her neck and died. Instead she broke her arm and walked home.

Their neighbor Carol came running down her lawn when Jackie walked past. Jackie's arm was just hanging dead. She couldn't hear anything Carol was saying. She thought she had gone deaf. Carol thought she was deaf, too. She kept snapping her fingers in front of Jackie's face. Clapping her hands. But when Jackie got home, and her mother opened the door, the sound came rushing back.

Ann doesn't know about the trees. She's seen the map in her friend's room, though. She comes over once in a while. Jackie told her it belonged to her mother. People stop asking questions when you bring up your dead mom.

Now, under the tree, Jackie squeezes Ann's hand and twists both their arms. Her fingers are wet and cold. Ann puts her other arm out for balance, but it isn't enough.

"Too little, too late, beautiful," Jackie says. She shouldn't have said that. Beautiful. Oh god. Her foot slips. Jackie can see exactly what's about to happen before it happens. The problem with fighting someone when you have your hands lashed to theirs is that when the loser falls, the winner falls, too.

They hit the gravel hard. Nothing breaks. Ann rolls over on her back, and Jackie does too, resting her head on Ann. They stay on the wet gravel, Jackie's head on Ann's stomach, both of them looking up at the tree.

Jackie and her mother came here on a picnic, after the hurricane. Her mother brought an old-fashioned wicker basket and lined it with a white sheet, like they were pretending to be a proper family in an old movie. They sat up on the hill over there. The city hadn't cleaned up the trees, yet. They sat near a huge fallen tree, laid out on its side, roots up into the air. All down the hill, trees were torn up and broken in half. People were wandering through the park with cameras, stopping to take pictures of each other standing by the biggest broken trees.

Her mother was wearing a dress. She never wore a dress, but that day she wore a dress and she packed a picnic basket and they sat up on the hill and watched everyone taking pictures.

"Your father brought me here on our first date," Jackie's mom said. Then she said, "I guess it wasn't really a date. But we came here, drunk, after the bars closed."

Down the hill, a man and a woman started yelling and fighting, and Jackie's mother spilled a bit of juice on the front of the dress.

"This would have been a better picnic with the trees," she said. "Do you ever wish that we'd lived out in the country? Did you like growing up in the city, Jackie?"

"I don't know," Jackie told her.

"I could have raised you out in the country. Maybe you would have been happier." She was quiet for a while, looking down at the tree roots and the dirt and the bright, exposed wood. Jackie just kept thinking about her mother and father, sitting here in the park, falling in love in the moonlight. How old were they? When was this?

Her mother took another drink of her juice.

"You have to go live with your father for a while," she said. "I'm sick."

But Jackie didn't go live with her father. She stayed with her mother.

Ann's stomach is making noises under her head, like she's hungry, and Jackie wants to reach up and touch Ann's face and her lips.

Ann doesn't say much at all. She's been quiet, today.

"Do you want to go on a date with me tonight, Ann?"

"What?" Ann doesn't sit up, at least. Jackie was worried that she would sit up. Or just walk away.

"We can do anything! This whole city is ours," Jackie says. "We can go to the carnival, or up the tower. We can find the old abandoned subway lines underneath the city. Don't go home. Come out on a date with me!"

Ann doesn't say anything for a long time, lying with Jackie's head resting warm on her stomach.

"I don't want to go home," Ann says.

16

The roller coaster creaks while it pulls them slowly up into the sky. There's a chain under their seats. You can hear it clicking. *Click click click.* Almost everything is wood when it ought to be metal. Wood cracks and breaks and splinters and warps, and Jackie can think of a hundred ways that wood will kill them. Ann and Jackie.

People die on these rides every year but they don't shut them down. They have a sign out front. *Use at your own risk.* Jackie squeezes Ann's hand.

"If we die," Jackie says, "I bet they don't even close the ride for a day."

This was Ann's choice for their date. Jackie still isn't even sure it is a date. Ann had to be talked into it. That's not how dates should be. She had to be talked into it, and Jackie should have just said, "Never mind."

Now Jackie can hear the attendants laughing about something. Greasy bastards. She can smell their cigarettes. They don't care what happens.

"If we die up here," Jackie says. "I am going to terrorize these people from beyond the grave."

okay

"I bet you killed her," Charlie says. "I bet when you were younger you murdered this poor woman and cut off her head, and now she's come back to expose you for the murderess you are."

"Oh, you caught me," Mrs. Richards says, shifting the laundry basket to her other hip. "You go call the police, and I'll try to get my laundry done and my affairs in order. I'm sure any minute they'll come to lock me up and throw away the key, based on the testimony of your pointing, headless ghost."

Mitchie was still facing the wall.

"Isn't she funny, Mitchie?" Charlie says. "Maybe we were wrong about old Mrs. Richards here. Maybe it was an accident about the girl dying. Maybe the poor girl heard one of Mrs. Richards' jokes, and she laughed her head off."

"Goodbye Charles." Mrs. Richards closes the door.

Charlie feels pretty good. Usually the old woman says something smart about Mitchie and slams the door before he can get a word in edgewise. Laughed her head off. He'll use that one again. Charlie reaches down to give his friend a scratch.

"A small victory, eh, Mitchie?"

The ghost follows them to the elevator, and it stands there while they wait. The dead girl isn't pretty. She probably wasn't pretty when her head was attached, either. She has a weird face, which looks even weirder because she keeps it completely expressionless. They wait for the elevator and she keeps talking the whole time, her lips moving soundlessly, dark with blood. Charlie closes his eyes to wait.

The elevator dings and Mitchie starts forward, tottering along. Inside, Charlie pushes the button to close the doors.

"No room, sorry," he says to the bloody, silent specter. She speaks again, moving her silent lips, and Charlie has a sick feeling in his stomach, watching the blood dribble out of her mouth. There are chunks of something in the dark blood, and her eyes roll back in her head.

Every goddamned day.

"Oh, walk it off," Charlie says to the ghost. The elevator doors slide closed.

Click click click. They're reaching the top. Right here they can unbuckle their seats and just keep rising. Jackie can feel it. She's dizzy. The sun is shining off the ocean. The air is cool. The clicking has stopped. Then the roller coaster is pulling them down and someone is yelling, "You assholes!" at the top of her lungs. "You assholes! You assholes!" Someone is laughing and yelling at the same time. Jackie is holding on to Ann.

The roller coaster shoves her to the side, slams Jackie into Ann. Slams Ann into Jackie.

"Oh," Ann says. It snaps them around another corner. It takes the corners so fast that they slam into the sides of their seats, elbows digging into each other, heads knocking together. Then they go up, and they come back down. Jackie's stomach is somewhere behind them.

Click click click, they pull into the little room where they started. Jackie and Ann climb out of their seats. The metal is cold in her hand and Jackie glares at the bored attendant who tries to help them. Greasy, laughing bastard.

"It's only four dollars if you go again," he says.

"Can we?" Ann says, but Jackie is so sore. "Come on Jackie," Ann says. "Maybe we'll die this time." Jackie shakes her head. "Maybe we'll die this time," Ann says again. "We'll be free."

"No," Jackie says.

"I thought you said we could do anything I wanted," Ann says, and there's a taunt in her voice that makes Jackie sick, like Ann knows that Jackie will do whatever she wants, like she has Jackie wrapped around her finger. This isn't a date, Jackie thinks. I'm so stupid.

Well, if it isn't a date, it isn't a date. Jackie doesn't know what to do on a date, anyway. And she's not wrapped around anyone's finger.

"I'm not getting on that roller coaster again," she says. She says it clearly. She thinks, I'm not a puppy dog.

"Let's find some payphones instead," Jackie says. She wants to get things back to normal. If this isn't a date, she has to act like she never thought it was. People don't hack phones on dates. They don't call up strange answering machines from payphones and try to guess their passwords.

Ann and Jackie leave each other secret messages. Everyone should have a hobby.

"Okay," Ann says. "I have the notebook."

They're working on a book called *The Hidden Guide to Telephones*. In a single day they can fill pages and pages of the notebook up with numbers, and each one gets a note.

1-800-555-0000	fax tone
1-800-555-0001	busy signal
1-800-555-0002	voicemail system

The girls already have a notebook half filled. They dial every one of these toll-free numbers, and write down who answers. If it's a business, they write the name of the business. If it's a voicemail computer system, they try to guess the passwords. Lots of people use the same passwords. 1111. 2222. 1234. 6789. If not, well, they take their time and they try everything else.

They call up Joe Business after he's gone home for the day, and his answering machine says, "If this is an emergency, you can reach me at my cell number," and they punch in his password and listen to the menu.

To change your outgoing message, press five.

"Hey, Squirrel, did I tell you what Ms. Garcia was wearing today?"

They call up Susan Politician, "If this is urgent, please call the switchboard at . . ." *To change your outgoing message, press five.*

"Bug, it's me. I'm sorry I haven't been in school. I've just been sick, that's all."

And that's their hobby. At first Jackie had all these rules. Never use the same payphone twice. Always dial with your knuckles so there are no fingerprints. Use fake names (Jackie was Bug, and Ann was Squirrel) and never call from a payphone near a video camera. But all those rules were useless. Nobody was ever going to arrest them. For what? For changing a politician's voicemail to an update about Ann's missed homework? For a recording of Jackie gushing about the length of Ms. Garcia's skirt?

Maybe those *are* crimes — imagine how great it would be to be on the run from the law with Ann. Holed up in cheap motels, pumping quarters into vibrating love beds and laughing at their terrible pictures on the news.

and

Jackie and Ann go looking for a payphone. Ann doesn't say much. Jackie's babbling. Has Ann been this quiet all night? She's just staring off, distracted. This isn't how you're supposed to behave on a date. Jackie is looking at the ground for coins while they walk. She's counting streetlights. She can't believe she wanted to tell Ann about her mother. She still wants to. She's so stupid. She knows this isn't a date. She knows that the smart thing would be to play it cool.

Ann is wearing torn jeans. They're dark and old. They make a weird sound when she walks. Jackie knows that she should play it cool, but she wants to reach out and hold her hand. She could make a trick of it. She could grab it and they could run. Jackie could pretend to read her palm. There are all sorts of reasons girls can touch.

"Come on! Let's go!" Jackie says, and she grabs Ann's hand, and they run. They run out into the street, down the stairs to the subway. Their voices echo, bouncing off the walls and getting louder with their laughter and Jackie's brain is echoing, too, happiness and fun and fear and chaos bouncing back and forth and amplifying until they are just screaming and running and laughing into the underground, pulling each other along. This is the first time she's seen Ann laugh in weeks. The subway trains are shaking the ground and the walls, until they finally have to stop to catch their breath by the turnstiles.

The big tiled walls down here are like the bathrooms at school. Jackie used to spend a lot of time staring at the tiles, waiting for Ann to finish getting ready after gym. She always finishes first. Jackie showers quickly and throws her clothes on. God knows what Ann is doing in there. Makeup, hair, and some secret ritual nobody ever taught Jackie. But she doesn't mind waiting. It's worth the wait.

So Jackie sits on the wooden bench and stares at the tiles, and she tries not to think about using her magic word. She could just whisper, "Mom," and she could slip into invisibility. Doesn't everyone want to be invisible in the girl's changing room? But then her mother would be behind one of those doors, glowing blue, dry heaving, clutching the toilet and saying, "Jackie. Jackie, I'm okay. Jackie, I didn't mean to wake you."

People are pushing through the turnstiles, but there's nowhere in particular that Jackie and Ann want to go. They stay underground until the rumble of another subway train fades, and then they head up to the street again. Ann leans against the railing. Jackie thinks, "Maybe I should get a pair of jeans like that. Something that shows off skin through rips, something sexy. I could get a whole new outfit. It would be a complete makeover. I could ask Ann." But she hasn't seen Ann wear makeup in weeks, either.

They walk, and Jackie is quiet, even though she wants to tell Ann about Ms. Garcia. Ms. Garcia is a stone-cold fox with bright diamond eyes. She takes no guff off anybody. In Jackie's English class, when a boy named Chris was flinging elastics, Ms. Garcia told him to grow up.

"Stupid bitch," Chris said under his breath, but everyone heard him.

Ms. Garcia smiled and she walked directly over to his desk

and she took hold of the two front corners. Their faces were very close. She said, "Wrong answer, Chris." And then she tipped him over backward, lifting the desk and chair back, and Chris fell out onto the floor with his books and pencils.

"You can't do that!" he yelled. He was almost crying. "You can't do that, you're a teacher!" Jackie couldn't take her eyes off the teacher. She looked so beautiful, standing above him like that. Strong.

Jackie stole a list of every teacher's phone number from the office. Ms. Garcia was right there on the first page. Kathy Garcia. Jackie won't ever have the guts to call her, though. What would she even say?

"Hello, Ms. Garcia. I am in your English class. My name's Jackie. I just wanted to say you were beautiful. And maybe we could go out to a movie. Whatever movie you want is okay with me."

Ann is looking at Jackie like she's just asked her a question and Jackie hasn't answered yet. This is a terrible date. Does Ann have new friends? Is that where she's spending all her time? Jackie is suddenly certain that she's losing her. She doesn't want to lose her. She doesn't want to spend less time together.

"Are you mad at me, Ann?" Jackie says. But Ann doesn't answer. They just walk in silence for a bit. Ms. Garcia is probably sitting at home wishing she could go to the movies. She is just waiting for the phone to ring. It is a little bit dark out. Soon the lights will come on. Jackie thinks, *I am useless.*

that

When Ann gets home, Margaret is sitting at the table, wrapping gauze around her hand too tightly. There is already blood seeping through the white material. Margaret looks up when her older sister comes in.

"Jesus!" Ann says, but Margaret just continues wrapping the gauze around her hand. "What happened? Are you alright?" Ann says. Her sister's blood is dark on the bandage. Oh god. Ann feels sick, looking at the blood. This is her fault. She was worried about the lives of hamsters and budgies.

"You were supposed to meet me after school," Margaret says. "You weren't there, so I came home. What do you think happened? She's hungry. She's getting hungrier and hungrier."

I

In her room, Martha Richards sets the laundry hamper down on the floor and lets out a long sigh. Charles and Mitchie are gone. Is the ghost still in the hallway? She thought she felt the cold again today, but maybe she's just fooling herself, maybe she's too credulous, like the people who go to see psychics.

Charles doesn't seem like a liar. Maybe he does see something there. Maybe it really is her daughter, trying to tell her something. But why can't Martha see her? What if this is some stupid, sick joke?

Every day, she pretends to be irritated. She acts like she doesn't believe. It's the only thing she can do. And afterwards, after the door closes, and Charles goes back upstairs with that idiot little dog of his, Martha stands there shaking. Every day. But holding the tears inside in front of Charles means she can't cry now, either, even when it's okay. She walks to the dresser and picks up the framed photograph of her daughter.

She didn't believe in any of this nonsense, at first. But day after day, here comes Charles, knocking on her door. Telling her about a girl standing right there, even though Martha can't see anything. She should have just shown him the photo on that first day, and asked him if it was her. But if he *is* lying he might have just said, "Oh yes, that's her." What if this is some cruel prank? What if Charles had somehow found out about the accident?

Martha Richards is no murderess. But of course it was her fault that Elizabeth died. Not a day goes by that she doesn't tell herself that it was her fault.

At three a.m. Charlie gives up trying to sleep. Whenever he closes his eyes, he can see that pale face with its open mouth. With his eyes closed, he is certain that the ghost is standing right there, beside the bed, her head down beside his, cradled in those bloodied hands. Her dark hair hanging down to the floor.

Mitchie's sitting at the foot of the bed. He can't sleep, either. He's looking up at Charlie with his cloudy-white eyes, his head crooked to the side. Charlie turns the light on beside the bed, and tries again to sleep. But as soon as his eyes are closed, there she is. Her mouth opening and closing, inches away from his face. No sound coming out. Plenty of blood, though.

On the telephone, Charlie's daughter Julia has a lot of opinions.

"The restless dead have unfinished business, Dad," she says, and Charlie rolls his eyes at Mitchie.

"Uh-huh," he says into the phone. "Restless business."

"Do you know what she wants from you?" Julia says.

"She wants me to bother Mrs. Richards every day, as far as I can tell. She wants me and Mitchie to go knock on her door and get the old girl all riled up."

"She's an unhappy spirit," Julia says. "She's carrying her own bloody head around in her arms. I think it's safe to say she wants you to do more than irritate Mrs. Richards. She wants revenge."

"Well, you haven't seen Mrs. Richards. It's pretty funny when she gets riled up," Charlie says. "Maybe the ghost thinks so, too. Maybe it's boring being dead."

"Fine, make jokes. When was the last good night's sleep you had, Dad?"

"How's your mom?" Charlie says. "Is she still seeing that doctor?" It doesn't do any good to talk about the ghost. They go around and around in circles. Julia is convinced that the thing wants him to kill Mrs. Richards. She thinks it is a vengeful spirit, but it doesn't seem so vengeful to Charlie.

Talking to Julia helps with the nightmares, though. They talk for another half hour, and then Charlie climbs back into bed. Mitchie comes up to flop down beside the pillow and with the dog's warm body beside him, Charlie finally falls asleep.

On his walk the next day, Mitchie attracts the attention of two young ladies who are on their way home from school. They come right over and the younger one crouches down next to Mitchie. Charlie can't get a break.

"I'm Ann," the older one says, holding her hand out for Charlie to shake. He shakes her hand, even though he doesn't want to. She's civilized, at least. "This is Margaret," Ann says. Margaret is smaller than Ann. And she's got bags under her eyes, like she's sick, or like she hasn't been sleeping.

Ann and Margaret. Charlie can't tell how old anyone is anymore. These girls are coming home from school, though. Sisters with dark hair. Julia kept her hair long like that, when she was their age. She cut it all off in high school, though. Mortified her mother.

"What's its name?" the younger girl, Margaret, asks, scratching Mitchie behind his ear. "Oh, it's old!" she says, looking back at her sister. Margaret scratches him again, and Mitchie loves it. Two minutes ago he couldn't even be bothered to wait for Charlie to finish his TV show. He had to go right now. Had to go out. Come on, Charlie. We have to go. We have to go. Scratch scratch at the door. But now Mitchie just wags his fat little tail, loving every minute of the attention. Stupid little bastard.

"Mitchie," Charlie says. "His name's Mitchie." The

older girl, Ann, is just staring at him. There's something a little spooky about the girls, but Charlie can't put his finger on it. Everything's spooky these days. A headless woman in the lobby, haunting them from beyond the grave. A creepy little girl isn't going to make much difference.

"It's old," Margaret says again, about Mitchie, and Charlie resists the urge to defend his friend's honor. Sure Mitchie's old. So what's wrong with that? "How long do dogs normally live, anyway?" she asks Charlie.

"You shouldn't talk to strangers," he tells the girl.

"Whatever," she says. She gives Mitchie one last scratch and then she stands up, and the two girls keep walking. Charlie watches them go, but Mitchie is already pulling on his leash toward the woods.

"You sure can pick 'em, Mitch," Charlie says.

The creepy girls are gone, and Charlie bends down to unhook Mitchie's leash. He watches his friend scramble up into the woods. The fat little dog can't run very well, but he gives it his all. He's old, sure, but get him out in the underbrush, and Mitchie takes off as fast as he can. He's still got plenty of life in him. Charlie's half certain that one of these days the little guy will run blindly into a tree trunk. *Thunk!* But it hasn't happened yet.

Mitchie runs out of sight, and Charlie lets him go. He stands there, listening to the sounds of traffic on the main road. Car, car, car, and the occasional bus. One of these days, he's gonna take Mitchie on a longer walk, like they used to go on. They'll walk up to the frog pond, by the water tower. Mitchie used to go nuts on the edge of the frog pond, when every few feet a startled frog would splash into the water. Or they could go down to the Northwest Arm. Mitchie could use some salt air. Probably they both could.

Charlie sits down on the wall that runs along the sidewalk, and he waits. When enough time has gone by, he calls out.

"Mitchie, come on."

He stands up, and wipes dust off his ass.

"Come on now, Mitchie, that headless monstrosity needs our help again today." Nothing.

"Mitchie, it's time to eat. Let's go!"

And finally there's a rustling in the bushes, and here comes Mitchie, sniffing the air, blinking those cloudy eyes, smiling at Charlie. Charlie bends down and hooks his leash on, and Mitchie pushes his warm, dry nose into Charlie's palm, and they start for home.

Today there's a bloody handprint on the glass of the front door. But the mailman is coming out just as they arrive, and he doesn't seem to see it. So Charlie figures it belongs to the ghost. And there she is.

On the other side of the glass, she holds her own head in her hands, as calm as ever. Her face is expressionless. Today her dress is dark with stains. Black stains around the neck, like her head had just been removed. This is new.

Mitchie is stuck in the corner again.

"Hey, look who it is," Charlie says. He gives a tug on the leash, trying to get Mitchie turned around. "Okay, we're ready," he says to her when they get inside. "Lead the way, madam." And Mitchie and Charlie follow her down the hall.

"Where do you suppose we're going today, Mitchie?" Charlie asks. "The vending machine? The TV room?" And when the ghost stops in front of room 135, he pretends to be surprised. "But, this is where Mrs. Richards lives!" he says. Mitchie sits down and tries to scratch himself behind the ear. Charlie knocks.

Mrs. Richards looks tired. She answers the door and she looks so tired that Charlie forgets the funny line he has prepared. He wishes he'd just left her alone today, or that he could reassure her, touch her shoulder, but the ghost is raising its arm, now, pointing at the woman with an incomprehensible certainty, and Charlie has no idea what to do but make jokes the way he always does.

"Good afternoon, Mrs. Richards," Charlie says. "Sorry

about all the barking last night. You know how Mitchie gets on a full moon." Mitchie's walking around in a slow circle now, at the end of his leash. He stops suddenly and he just falls over on his side for a nap. No grace at all, that dog.

"I didn't hear any barking last night," Mrs. Richards says.

"Well, you're one of the lucky ones," Charlie tells her. "He's a little hellion, that one." He looks down at his dog, to make his point, and he can't help smiling at the sight of Mitchie's tongue all rolled out of his head. Poor little bastard. All tuckered out from his run in the woods. "Anyway, I'm here about the headless pointing woman," Charlie said. "You probably guessed. She is there every day when I come back from my walk, and she leads me down the hallway to your door and right now she's just standing there pointing at you. You know I wouldn't bother you about this, except it is *every day* that this has been happening."

"What do you want me to do about it?" Martha Richards says. "I mean, really, Charles. That sounds like a personal problem." But she doesn't close the door like usual. She's looking where Charlie said the ghost was, like she wants to see her, but can't.

The next day, Margaret and Ann wait in the woods.

"Please . . ." Ann says, "we don't have to do this." She picks at one of the tears in her jeans. She has no idea when they tore. It doesn't matter. "We can just buy some rats or something at the pet store."

"With what money?" Margaret says. She clears her throat. "Rats are too small anyway."

Here comes Mitchie, trotting along. Margaret crouches and holds her hand out for him like she has food. He hasn't noticed the girls yet.

"Hey dog," Margaret says, and his ears perk up when he hears her voice. She's got a burlap sack in her other hand. Margaret coughs suddenly. She clears her throat. Then clears it again. She swallows.

"You are not okay," Ann says.

"I'm fine," her sister says. "Just let it go." Mitchie is smiling now, panting. "Here, fella," Margaret calls. And when Mitchie gets close enough, Margaret takes the burlap sack and she scoops him up. In the sack, Mitchie doesn't know what's going on. He doesn't know he's being stolen. It feels like he's being hugged. His fat little tail just wags harder.

her

When Mitchie doesn't come back from the woods, Charlie goes in after him. He walks around in circles for an hour, calling out for his stupid dog. At first he's sure that Mitchie just hasn't heard him.

"Mitchie! God damn it. Mitchie!" And then Charlie thinks maybe old Mitchie found two trees pressed up against each other and got stuck in the corner where they met. That happened once.

But after a while, Charlie gets to thinking that maybe Mitchie just found somewhere to fall down and die. He doesn't want to think this, but there it is. That day has been coming. Charlie knows it. He's known it for a while. But he likes to think that it's coming for the both of them.

And Mitchie wouldn't just die somewhere off in the woods. He'd want to be with Charlie. He would wait until it was just him and Charlie somewhere, and he would die with his snout in Charlie's hand.

After an hour of yelling and walking in circles, Charlie goes home. Maybe Mitchie's back there now, stuck in the corner outside the front door. Charlie can already picture his friend stuck in the corner like always, and he walks faster. The building is lit up in the early evening sunset, and he knows Mitchie is waiting there for him. Charlie gets to the door and pulls it open. But there's no Mitchie in the lobby. There's no Mitchie inside, either. Only that headless thing.

The ghost is standing in the doorway, already moving its mouth, but Charlie walks right past. There is no way he's going to follow it down the hall to Mrs. Richards' room. She always has something to say about Mitchie. She always has some opinion. And Charlie doesn't want to hear it. The ghost follows him to the elevator, but he ignores it.

The doors open, and he steps inside, alone.

"God damn it, Mitch," Charlie says.

Ann and Jackie meet outside of school, before the first bell. Ann looks like she hasn't slept in days. She doesn't have her backpack. She's wearing those same torn jeans.

"I can't go in," Ann says. She looks like she wants to say more, but she doesn't. Jackie doesn't know what to do. Did she go too far, asking Ann out? Is that why she's upset?

"Why not?" Jackie says.

Ann shrugs her shoulders. "Let's do something else," she says.

So they get back on the bus and go downtown. On the bus, Ann just looks out the window. She doesn't say anything. Well, that won't do. Jackie is determined to show her a good time.

Downtown Jackie sees the cop who arrested her. He's crossing the street, and doesn't see her. Jackie takes Ann's hand.

"I have an idea," she says. They find a drugstore.

When the cop who arrested Jackie walks underneath them, Jackie's ready. He has his hat in his hand like a real gentleman, and the two girls are on the pedestrian bridge, perched like squirrels. He is all alone. Jackie is not afraid.

"Hey officer!" she calls. He stops and squints up, shielding his eyes against the sun. He smiles blindly, and Jackie lifts the bag of water balloons up by the bottom and dumps them down toward his head. They're all different colors, red and green and yellow and blue and white, and they fall in slow motion. God knows what he must be thinking.

It must look like a miracle.

"Eat it!" Jackie yells.

They burst against his face. They burst on his shoulder and his arms. He drops his hat. Jackie and Ann run like hell. They find an office building with a huge revolving door, and they push into it together. Jackie is laughing. They run up the escalator, pushing past men and women who can't stop frowning in their ugly suits.

"Oh, hello, Janet. How was your vacation?"

"Not long enough, Steve. Not long enough."

Upstairs, they push the button for the elevator, and then they wait calmly. Ten. Nine. Eight. The elevator is taking its time, but there's no rush. It was the perfect crime. It was the right spot to hit the cop. He had no way to chase them. Ann doesn't look scared, either.

"Lovely weather, don't you think?" Jackie says to a tall woman in a delivery uniform. She has small gold earrings that Jackie thinks are subtle and very nice.

"Oh yes," she says. They ride the elevator up with her.

"Lovely weather," Jackie says again to the delivery woman. That's just about the extent of her business-person water-cooler vocabulary. She tries to think of something else. "Annual reports!" Jackie laughs. "Liquidation! Annual shareholders!" She can't stop laughing. She puts her face against the wall and she just shakes. The delivery woman smiles.

"Stock options," the delivery woman says. "Severance packages. Resume cv cover letters."

"Libel suit!" Jackie says.

Then the door is open again. It is time to run like hell again. Across pedways, into other buildings, into the mall, down through the parking lot. They make their way to the park.

They're just like everyone else, now. They're blocks away, and out of breath. So they sit down under the hanging branches of a tree.

"Eat it!" Jackie says. "Oh man." It was so perfect. She feels good again. It feels good to run. The sun is shining and there's a cool breeze on her face. On days like this, it doesn't seem real that she sometimes sees her mother's ghost. It doesn't seem so bad. It fades like a bad dream. The world is bright and warm and soft and green. The school year is almost over. Two squirrels are chasing each other around a tree trunk like maniacs.

There's a big group of pigeons and Jackie climbs up on top of a picnic table. The pigeons are all pushed together, fighting for a slice of pizza. Jackie jumps up into the air, with her wings out wide. Look at that wingspan!

"Caw caw!" she yells in midair, and they all take flight at once. Jackie has the largest wingspan. She is the queen of the pigeons. That pizza slice is hers, if she wants to claim it, but it's enough to know that she could. She sits back down. Ann isn't laughing or smiling. She looks tired again.

A woman with a small child comes over and stands in front of Jackie.

"Why did you have to scare those pigeons?" she says. "Did that make you feel big? Did it make you feel strong? Don't you have any respect? We have to share the world with nature, you know." And it seems like she's saying all this as much for her son, who is chewing his thumb, as for Jackie. But before Jackie can reply, Ann is laughing. She laughs and laughs, and when the woman tries to say something else, Ann only laughs harder.

too.

Ann has come over to do homework, but they haven't been to school, so there's no homework today. The two girls wait until Jackie's father is in his study, reading, and then they get their jackets on. First the left arm, then the right arm. It feels like everything is important. Today's the day. Tonight's the night. Jackie is going to get the girl, even though she's the awkward teen. She's the nerdy virgin in a sex comedy who only wants kisses.

They go down the block to rent a movie from the corner store. They want something chock full of sex and nudity and adult themes which may not be suitable for minors. This is a sleepover, and sleepovers mean gratuitous nudity. This is what you learn from the movies.

The boy behind the counter has his hair tucked behind his ears, which makes them stick out. That is his identifying, quirky character trait. When Jackie and Ann put the movie down on the counter, he doesn't notice the title at first. He opens the case, scans the disc on the computer and then looks up. He looks back at the title.

"Uh," he stammers. "are either of you eighteen?" He won't look directly at them.

Jackie purses her lips like the girl on the movie cover. "It's nothing we can't handle, I assure you," she says.

He pushes his hair back behind his ear again.

Back at Jackie's building, Ann takes the elevator and

Jackie races up the stairs to the apartment. She loves running up stairs. It feels so perfect, reaching each landing, grabbing the railing and swinging herself around the turn, flinging herself up the next set of stairs.

She comes laughing in the door. Her father looks like he wants to ask where they've been, but his daughter is laughing and safe, and he looks relieved. Ann sits down to pull her boots off, and Jackie gives him her best perfect-daughter smile.

"Can Ann stay over tonight?" she asks him.

"If her mother says that it's okay."

Ann says nothing.

In bed Ann and Jackie look up at the ceiling and lie on their backs like teen girls are supposed to do, and Jackie does all the talking. Ann keeps going quiet and Jackie feels like the day is almost over, which isn't what she wants. So she rolls over on her side and she puts her hand on Ann's shoulder and she kisses her friend on the forehead and then on the nose and then Jackie kisses Ann on the lips. She's gone off the script, here. This isn't the way this scene in the movie was supposed to go. Jackie was supposed to squeal with delight and do Ann's hair and they were going to have girl talk all night and eat chocolate ice cream right out of the carton, but instead, she goes ahead and puts her mouth on Ann's, and Ann doesn't kiss her back. She doesn't say anything or react at all. Jackie doesn't know what to do. So she starts talking.

She talks about the first girl she ever kissed, Laura. Laura had pictures of horses everywhere in her room. She had magazine pages of dogs and kittens torn out and hung up. She had a house with a big tree and a tire swing right out front.

Why would Ann care how Laura's room was decorated? She hasn't said anything yet, though. Maybe she's still waiting for Jackie to squeal and break out the chocolate ice cream so they can talk about boys. Jackie keeps talking instead. Her hand is still on Ann's shoulder, but she doesn't know what else to do with it.

Laura had pictures from magazines up everywhere. She had a big poster of bats. Scientific names of bats. Snub-noses. So many types of bats. Back then Jackie thought it was creepy, but talking about it now she realizes that Laura was kind of awesome. She was a huge nerd and she just didn't care. Jackie never even knew there were that many types of bats. Laura's older sister, Kelly, was on the same soccer team in elementary school as Jackie. Kelly was the biggest girl on the team, tall and muscled. She was the loudest girl, too, and the most popular. Jackie wanted to be her friend. Everyone did.

Laura was a year and a half younger, with long blonde hair and glasses. She interrupted her sister's parties to show everyone the newest issue of some scientific journal. She got so excited about things like sonar, and she just couldn't understand why nobody else got excited. She wanted her sister's approval, too.

And everyone teased her. It was just one more way to impress her sister. They threw popcorn at Laura, and "accidentally" spilled their drinks on her dress. They hid her science magazines and replaced them with porn Kelly stole from their dad. Jackie teased her, too.

And then, at one party, Kelly locked Laura and Jackie in an attic crawlspace together. She locked them in and sat outside with her back to the door, laughing. Jackie could hear another voice, then another, until the whole soccer team was out there laughing. They had planned this.

Laura and Jackie sat in the dusty crawlspace in silence while everyone laughed outside. Laura was crying, but she was always crying. There was a big crowd outside the door, chanting, "Seven minutes in heaven. Seven minutes in heaven."

And Jackie knew that afterward, everyone was going to

tease them anyway. These were her friends. She knew them. So she decided, brushing dust off her jeans, that she might as well.

"They're going to make fun of us anyway," she said, and Laura just looked at her. Jackie leaned forward and touched the younger girl's face. She stopped crying.

"Are you okay?" Jackie said, and Laura nodded. And then Jackie kissed her. Kissing girls comes easy, like breaking windows. Jackie grabbed Laura and pulled her close and she kissed her on the lips. Outside Kelly was laughing and leading the chant.

Ann still hasn't said anything. Jackie's never told anyone this before, but a woman should be brave. She sits back a little, and takes her hand off Ann's shoulder. They're sitting too close maybe.

Jackie's first kiss was exciting, and dangerous, but no secret. Laura told everyone, when they let the two girls out, and Jackie just laughed. Kelly was going to tease her? She planned to taunt Jackie and call her a lesbian? Well, Jackie kissed her little sister. What would Kelly say at school, then? Jackie is a lesbian? Yes, Kelly, Jackie and your little sister Laura are lesbians together.

She wants to tell Ann about the look on Laura's face after their kiss, half shocked, but half dreamy. Or about the letter that Laura wrote her years later, from the far-off city where she was living now. She wants Ann to have that dreamy look on her face now, too, but Ann hasn't got any look at all.

Ann gets up, grabs her backpack, and runs out of the room.

29

Margaret is at the bathroom sink, trying to be quiet. Ann is going to hear her if she doesn't stop coughing. Margaret coughs again and then again and something wet and red hits the porcelain. She doesn't look too closely. She washes it down the drain, and then she fills her hands with the cool water and splashes her face. She can breathe again. It was nothing. Ann would only worry.

part 2

This part takes place one month later

30

It's a school day, but that doesn't really mean anything anymore. There's work to be done. In the back of the paper, someone is giving away kittens. Free to a good home. Some days Ann had to go all the way downtown, but today there's a whole litter just over by the mall. On the phone, she tries not to ask if the kittens are plump.

Then she puts on one of her mother's dress shirts, and clean pants. She puts on her nice shoes. In the mirror she sure looks like she comes from a good home. A decent sort of country girl. Her sister Margaret starts howling downstairs in her locked room when she hears Ann at the front door. She hasn't eaten, and she recognizes the sound of the locks. Margaret knows where Ann is going, even if she doesn't understand anymore that it's her sister. Food. Locks mean food. The door means food. Everything is connected with food.

Sometimes Ann tells herself that there's a moral difference between killing kittens for no reason and what she does. Killing kittens just to kill kittens would be evil. That would be cruel for cruelty's sake. But Margaret needs to be fed. This is the sort of thing that a real country girl would have to do. It's practical, not evil. People kill animals for food all the time.

And Ann can't stand the way Margaret gets when she hasn't eaten. Most of the time, it's easy to remember that she isn't really Ann's sister anymore. She's something else. She grunts and howls and makes animal sounds. But after a few days without food, she starts finding words. Always random words, like accidents, but they come out in Margaret's voice.

The mall is down near the water. Ann forgot they were doing construction. She doesn't get out enough. This is all going to be a parking lot soon. That's what the big sign says.

The yacht club is right there. She could just take a boat and go. There's something about the smell of the salt air that makes a person feel free. But her sister needs to be fed, and she has an address scribbled down. So, Ann is practical. She's a good country girl. She does what needs doing.

When the stranger opens the door Ann sees a baby gate across the doorway. There's a formula bottle on the counter, and a blanket on the floor. The woman's got a kid in one arm, and you can bet there are more in the house somewhere, in behind the walls maybe.

Ann fakes a lovely smile for the woman and she gets into character. Oh my goodness what an adorable baby. Oh my goodness look at these kittens. Have you ever seen anything so adorable? Couldn't you just eat them up?

"We didn't think we'd find someone willing to take them," The woman with the baby says. "Not this quickly, anyway." Her baby is spitting up on her. "Are you sure your mother's okay with this?" she says. Ann smiles. The woman wipes at the vomit a bit, but misses half of it. It just sits there on her shoulder.

"We're in town today to see my uncle," Ann says. The trick is to keep touching the kittens. Keep your hands on them all the time, like you can't get enough. Aren't they wonderful? It makes you look tender. "My mom and I have a place out in the country. There's mice in the house at this time of year, and these guys will have plenty to keep themselves busy." It's important to talk to the kittens, too. "Won't you?" Ann says. "Won't you be busy? Chasing little mousies!"

"They're great, aren't they?" the woman says.

"Is this all of them?" Ann asks.

The black kitten doesn't like Ann at all. All the other ones are as stupid as this woman, rolling around like they can't even remember to stand up. But this black kitten is looking at Ann like he's heard about her.

"That sounds really nice," the woman says. "Living on a farm like that. Do you want a glass of juice or something?"

Ann brought a carrier with her, and she starts dropping the kittens inside, one by one. The black kitten tries to escape, to climb out of the cardboard box. When she gets her hand around him, he bites her. This is not going to be enough. They're so scrawny. The woman is still smiling at Ann from the doorway, bouncing her plump little baby on her shoulder.

"Maybe a glass of lemonade," Ann says. They go into the kitchen, and Ann feels right at home. It is time to be practical here. You have to put food on the table, and these kittens are too small. That baby has got way more meat.

There's a knife on the counter, laid on the cutting board, like farm equipment.

had

31

Ann gets back outside and everything is so bright and open. Everyone is busy going to work. Coming home from work. The carrier is heavy in her hand, and the kittens are mewling. The baby, too. They don't like the sound of the cars. And when she peeks inside, the black kitten is just looking back at her. She likes him, she realizes. He doesn't trust her at all, and it makes her like him.

Back at the house, Ann locks the door behind her, and the kittens and the baby are still making noise. Margaret can hear them from her room, and it drives her crazy. She can hear them and now she is pounding on the wall. Ann looks through the peephole, into her sister's room. The chains look solid. So she opens the door and goes in.

The kittens are quiet now. They can hear Margaret, and have no idea what to make of those sounds. The baby keeps crying, of course. It isn't as smart as the animals. It doesn't have the instincts. Margaret hasn't eaten in two days, and she is desperate. The words are coming.

"Homework lonely makeup mother ice cream," she says, and the words sound wrong. Ann doesn't look at her. Right beside the door is a CD player, ready with Margaret's shitty music, and Ann presses play. The volume is up full blast.

Then Ann opens the top of the carrier, and reaches in for the fat arms of that woman's baby. She sets him down on the floor, and pushes him with her foot to where her sister can reach. She pulls out the mewling white kitten, then the grey. The other white one.

Outside in the hall, she leans her back against the door. The music is so loud that it drowns everything else out. The kitten carrier is on the floor beside her, and inside it, the black kitten is still sitting. He looks like he expects her to pull him out, too, and toss him into that room, but she doesn't.

He's wrong about her. He ought to look grateful. Inside the room, though, Margaret is getting louder. You can hear her over the music now. More words.

There's blood on her shoes and Ann feels a bit sick. She doesn't like the words, but after a while Margaret calms down and the music is the only noise again. The little black kitten is mewling and Ann closes her eyes and pretends she is just home from school. Her sister Margaret has the music up too loud, even though she knows Ann has to study. As soon as Mom gets home, Margaret'll turn it down. Of course.

But what can you do? You can't just tell on her, she'll deny it. She's so aggravating. Look at her, look at the look on her face, behind Mom's back. Smug and self-satisfied. Human.

32

In the morning, Ann wakes up on the couch thinking that she's just fallen asleep. She thinks it's late afternoon. She's had a nap after school. Her mother is in the kitchen, cooking macaroni and cheese for her and Margaret. Everything is right for a few seconds, but dreams don't last. Their mother hasn't come back to them.

The morning newspaper has a picture of that woman on the cover. Ann sits down to read it on the front step, with the kitten on her lap. It's the cover story and they are aghast, downtown in newspaperland. Aghast! A young single mother, murdered! And her baby has been kidnapped. It doesn't mention the kittens at all.

"They don't mention you at all, Jackie," she tells him, but he doesn't seem offended. What does he care? In the kitchen she opens a can of wet food for him, and he perks up when he hears the sound, like Margaret when she hears the door. Ann wishes her sister would eat wet cat food. But they tried that with their mother, back before their mother got loose. They tried that first. Then they tried raw steaks. Bloody. It still wasn't fresh enough.

After breakfast, the kitten follows her down the stairs, padding along the hallway to Margaret's room. Darling little sister Margaret will still be sleeping. She was up all night, howling and upturning furniture. But it's quiet time, now. Ann unbolts the door, and pulls it open. She puts the bucket down, and she cleans up as best she can.

There's blood everywhere except a big half circle, where Margaret's chains let her reach to lick the floor. But out past where the chains extend, there is blood, and there are chunks of kitten. Chunks of the poor missing baby. Margaret is curled up in the corner, and she looks peaceful. Her shirt is ripped, and underneath it, you can see the holes, where their mother took her organs. She isn't breathing, either, but she is pawing at the floor, lost in some dream. The trick is not to look at her face.

Her face is bent out of shape, but still recognizable. There are too many teeth in her mouth, now. It is torn open at the sides. Split along her cheeks, so the weird, jagged stones of her teeth can breathe. It would be better if it was just a twisted mess of a face, but it still looks like Margaret. The mouth has split in a small twist on the left side, like her old smile.

When it was their mother chained in the corner like this, Margaret and Ann would argue. This was when she was still Margaret. But Ann didn't mind the arguing. At least, when they were fighting about it, they were sisters. It was just the two of them, taking care of the thing their mother had become. Only, they couldn't agree about how exactly they should care for her.

The first time they gave their mother a live animal to eat it was a dog they stole. Mitchie. He was from the apartment building down the street. They used to see him all the time, on their way to school and back. Every day, he went out for a walk with his old man owner, and every day Mitchie would run into the woods. He was old, and he couldn't run very fast. But he would run into the woods anyway.

Ann and Margaret would walk home from school, and that old man would be standing there at the edge of the woods, stooped over, hollering and hollering. "Mitchie, you get out here right now. God damn it, Mitchie." And eventually Mitchie would come stumbling out of the woods. They were cranky, blind old men together.

When the two girls realized that their mother needed live food, Ann wanted to buy birds from the pet store. Or maybe they could try to trap pigeons, she said. They were animals but they weren't pets, you know? They weren't a part of someone's family.

"Do you know how hard it would be to catch a pigeon?" Margaret said.

So they came home with Mitchie, and they put him in the room with their mother and ran upstairs to get away from the sounds. Ann turned on the TV, as loud as it would go.

They didn't talk about it until late that night when Margaret knocked on her sister's door and climbed into the bed. She put her head on Ann's shoulder and she said, real quiet, "Do you think he's still out there calling for Mitchie?" And in the morning, Ann woke up early to clean up what was left of Mitchie so that Margaret wouldn't have to see.

Now there's no arguing. There's nobody to argue with. Margaret will wake up when the sun goes down, and soon Ann will have to feed her again. Right now, Ann just wants to sleep some more, but there's always more work. She has to clean this up. The kitten sits in the doorway and watches as Ann cleans up drying chunks of baby, and he yawns.

just

Jackie puts her hand on the walrus and she can hear the warm, rushing blood. She doesn't know if it is a boy or a girl. A girl maybe. Her blood is warm. Her eyes are full of blood and she is pink pink pink. She's staring at Jackie with those eyes, and Jackie is smiling at the zoo security guard like she's not terrified. The guard is yelling something or other.

"*Blah blah blah,*" he yells. "*Blah blah blah blah.*" Jackie's classmates are crowded around him now, watching her. She looks crazy up here, but they're the ones who think that a little fence like that can stop them. Her teachers look tired, but they are always tired.

Well, Jackie has decided that she's not going back to school today. No prison can hold her! There is a whole entire world out there that she can see, but every day all she sees are the same classrooms and the same hallways, all day long. Her mother did just fine without high school. Jackie can get a tire iron, too.

The walrus is still looking.

She stands on the edge of the walrus pool and waves goodbye to her classmates; she will never see them again and it is polite to wish them well. But mostly they just stare at her blankly, like they're lined up in front of the sea cucumber tank. Jackie is not a sea cucumber, though. She waves to a mother and a little boy. She waves especially to a little pink girl. Pink hat. Pink dress. The little pink girl points her finger at Jackie, so Jackie makes a funny face just for her. The little girl shrieks with laughter. The boy laughs, too. For one second Jackie is a hero up here. For one second she feels like even crazy people can be heroes.

And Jackie jumps into the water. It goes up her nose and right into her brain and then everything is white. Her eyes hurt and she can hear people whispering. Jackie rolls onto her side and throws up on someone's feet. A man leans down next to her and puts his hand on her back.

"You're okay," he says. "You swallowed a lot of water."

Everyone is standing too close. Jackie throws up more water. The light is so bright. She is beside the walrus tank now, sitting in a puddle of thrown-up water. Everyone is crowded around her, but nobody good. She can't see the little pink girl or her family. She can't see Ann. The paramedic pats Jackie on the back again.

"I'm okay," she tells him. "I'm okay. Go back to bed. I didn't mean to wake you."

34

Ms. Garcia can't keep still. She keeps asking, "Are you warm enough?" Jackie is wrapped in three blankets, sitting with her back against the wall in the security office. She's more than warm enough, but she likes when Ms. Garcia asks. They called Jackie's father more than an hour ago. They're waiting.

"Are you sure she doesn't need a doctor?" Ms. Garcia asks the security guard again. He shrugs his shoulders, which isn't an answer at all.

"I have to go do my rounds," he says, after a few more minutes. "I'll be back."

"We'll hold our breath," Ms. Garcia says, and then he's gone. It's just the two of them now, sitting in the office and waiting. The other students and teachers are all gone. She's very beautiful.

"You're very beautiful," Jackie says. It could be the sort of thing that a scared girl says, when she sees another woman being strong. But it isn't, not the way Jackie says it. She says it very clearly, and very simply, and Ms. Garcia's face flushes with surprise. She doesn't answer, and she turns away to check her phone, but not before Jackie sees the smile.

Then Jackie's father is in the doorway. He wraps his arms around Jackie and kisses her on the top of her head.

On the way home, her father doesn't say anything for

a long time. When they get home, he comes around to open the door.

"I was going to take us out to a movie tonight," he says. "If you're still up for it."

"I'm not in trouble?" Jackie says.

"What good would it do?" he says. He shakes his head. He's not smiling, and she can't tell whether he's angry or not. "You are your mother's daughter, Jackie."

She loves him for saying that.

35

Jackie stands under the department store's enormous sign. She remembered the name, even though her aunt only said it one time on the telephone to someone else. This is the department store where Jackie's mother worked. Whenever she goes to her broken-arm tree or any of her trees, she thinks about this department store.

There's a mother and daughter here, too. They are standing outside one of the big picture windows, looking in at the elaborate display. The little girl has a fancy scarf wrapped around her neck with little pink pom-poms dangling down from the ends.

"How do they make them fly?" the little girl says. She swings around to look at her mom, and the pom-poms whip through the air. Her mom points up at something in the window.

"They use wires," the mom tells her. "Look, you can see them." Jackie looks, too, and there they are, little wires ruining the illusion. The little girl has her face pushed up against the window now, straining to see. She's up on her tiptoes.

"Oh," says the little girl. She sounds disappointed.

"No they don't," Jackie says. "It's magic, how they fly like that. It's a miracle."

"But I can see the wires," the little girl says. Her mother doesn't say anything, she just stares at Jackie. "Look, you can see the wires," the girl says.

"Those are puppet strings," Jackie says.

"Puppet strings?"

"Yeah. There are people who live up in the ceiling there. That's all they do all day, is make those mannequins dance and fly."

"What do they eat?" she says. Her mother is already pulling her away.

"They eat children," Jackie says, and the little girl gasps. She puts the scarf over her face in little pink horror. Then she's being pulled away. Mom to the rescue. The little girl looks back at Jackie, and Jackie gives her a small wave.

"I'm here to visit my dead mom!" Jackie yells after them.

36

All night Ann hears her down there, screaming and thrashing. Margaret needs to be fed again. The little black kitten doesn't like those sounds at all, and he burrows under Ann's arms. Margaret needs to be fed. But Ann can't do it tonight. Tomorrow night. Margaret'll be screaming and crying and she'll start to use words again. This is what always happens.

She'll say, "Ann," in the middle of some string of random words. That will be too much. And Ann will be right back out there, finding her little sister something to eat. But not tonight. Tonight she sits with the kitten in her lap, and she tries to remember the words to old songs while Margaret screams. When she falls asleep, she dreams that she can remember all the words perfectly.

Ann wakes up with the kitten pushing his cold little snout into her neck.

"Oh, hello," she says. "Good morning, Jackie." She feeds him in the kitchen, and makes herself some breakfast. She sets him and his dish on the kitchen table, and sits in her usual seat. It's good to have someone to eat with.

"Slow down," she tells him.

Downstairs, she pulls open the door, so she can watch Margaret sleep, and the air inside is cold. Too cold. The window is open, and Ann feels this rush of excitement. Maybe her sister got out. Maybe it's over.

But Margaret hasn't escaped. She's right there, on the floor, curled up in their mother's arms. Their mother's face is twisted and bloody, and there's fur on the floor from whatever they ate last night. It's a mess of blood and bone and strips of flesh. And they're sleeping peacefully, wrapped around one another. They look so calm and quiet.

Ann doesn't know what to do. She could chain her mother up now. But then what? Then she's taking care of two of them. It's hard enough finding food for Margaret. Their mother is bigger. She needs more food. And when will it end? How long will she have to go on hunting for them?

While Ann watches, Margaret nuzzles her torn, jagged face into their mother contentedly, and makes a sound almost like a cat purring. Something inside Ann flips like a switch.

She takes the kitten upstairs, and she opens the front door and sets him outside.

"You should go," she tells him, and he just sits there. "Go," she says again. But it's not her problem. She closes the door. He'll leave eventually. And if he doesn't, well, he's small enough that he might go unnoticed.

Ann goes back downstairs, into her sister's room. She unlocks Margaret's chains while her sister and her mother sleeping. The window is still open, and when night falls, there'll be nothing keeping anyone locked inside. They look peaceful. Ann doesn't know why she's so angry. Fear?

She kicks her sister in the ribs.

"Hey Margaret," she says.

She kicks her again, and the eyes open.

"Hungry?" Ann says.

The display windows of the department store are amazing, but so is the rest of the building. There are big rock gargoyles up high, looking down at everyone like they're food. The stone front of the building is carved into whirls and waves and spirals. It's so smooth and round, Jackie wants to put her ear against it and hear the ocean. There's a man in a bright red uniform with shiny buttons; he's right inside the front door and he wants to know how he can help.

"Can you direct me to ladies' gloves, fine sir?" Jackie says. He smiles and steps away from the wall. He pulls open the second inside door with a clean, white-gloved hand, and there is a rush of sweet-smelling air from inside. He bows. Jackie curtsies. It's all very civilized.

"First floor, miss," he says. "Just through here." Big double doors and then six red-carpeted steps leading up into the department store. The ceiling plays quiet piano music. This is the soundtrack to her mother's old life. Or maybe they had actual piano music, a man in a tuxedo, playing gently all day long. In Jackie's head, her mother lived in a golden age.

And she can't help it: she imagines that she is her mother, walking to work. She's thinking her thoughts.

"Oh, I hate coming here," Jackie's mother thinks. "Work work work, selling ladies' gloves to rich old women. At least I have a beautiful daughter at home. Oh so pretty.

She could use a gift. Today I will buy her something beautiful. Today I will quit smoking."

The gloves are on display in long glass cases. They're beautiful, but Jackie does not care to look at them. She likes the weird wallpaper pattern here. The brown colors they use. It looks ancient, but elegant. She likes the low-hanging light fixtures. She doesn't like the woman behind the counter, though. The woman behind the counter has long teeth.

"Did you know Patricia?" Jackie asks, and nobody answers her. "She used to work here." She steps forward, pretends to trip, and she slams a fist into glass. It doesn't break, and pain shoots up her arm. Before she thinks about what she's doing, she slams the fist into the case again. Again and again.

This isn't what Jackie had in mind when she decided to come here today.

She pounds the case as hard as she can with her fist. Then someone has their arms around Jackie from behind, pulling her back from the case that won't break. The woman behind the counter has her hand over her mouth in shock. Someone, old and strong beside her, walks Jackie back toward the entrance.

"I don't normally . . ." Jackie says.

"You don't normally what?" the stranger asks. She has a quiet voice, and Jackie is afraid to look directly at her. She feels certain that it's her mother walking beside her, older now, old and wrinkled and at the end of a long life. That's not a normal thing to worry about, and so Jackie is worried about having that worry, too.

Two girls walk by in school jackets.

"Oh my god!" one of them says, and she stops right in front of Jackie and the stranger. She's younger than Jackie. She's got thick, dark eyebrows. She's so pretty. If Jackie asked her, she'd probably be her friend. They'd have so much fun, talking about all the boys who like her. "Does that hurt?" she says.

"Does what hurt?" Jackie looks her right in the eye.

"Your hand," the girl says. She reaches out for it, but Jackie pushes past her. The strange old lady still has her arm linked with Jackie's.

"It's changing color," the girl says. "I think you need to see a doctor."

You know who would be really good teammates in a fight? Jackie and Ann. There's no way you could take them both out. They would be the ultimate fighting team. The odds of both being unconscious at the same time are very slim. The odds of you knocking one of them unconscious and surviving the ensuing berserker rage of the other? Perhaps even more slim.

"Are you okay?" the old woman asks. Jackie stops and looks at her, finally. This old lady cannot possibly be her mother. "Are you listening? You should go to a hospital. Can I call your parents? Do they know where you are?" She won't stop talking. Jackie pulls her arm away and stumbles out into the road. The woman is back there, still talking. Jackie spins around to say something, and for a second it really does look like her mother.

"Mom?" Jackie says. The world around her flickers when she says the word.

A car hits Jackie.

Glass shatters.

listened

part 3

**In which Jackie doesn't realize
she's been hit by a car**

to

38

Mrs. Hubert won't be calling her *dear* again anytime soon.
Jackie's Sunday best gave her the wrong impression. She
thought Jackie was one of those proper young ladies from
her church, but Jackie is one of those proper young ladies
you see on the TV news at night.

Smash!

Now there are two big rocks in the car. There's broken
glass everywhere. *Smash!* Jackie loves that sound. All her
arm hair is standing up. Her mouth tastes like blood. When
you open the cat food can and the cat jumps right up from
whatever it was doing, that's how breaking glass sounds to
Jackie. Perfect. Amazing.

Jackie leans in through the window of Mrs. Hubert's
car and brushes the glass off the passenger seat rock with
her good hand. She pulls the seat belt across and fastens it
securely. This is nice. It paints a pretty picture. Out for a
Sunday drive with the windows down. Mister and Missus
Rock. Lovely.

There are no tree limbs scattered in the backyard. The
grass is green and freshly mowed, but the tree branches
are gone. There are no trees at all in the backyard. There
are holes where each tree used to be. Jackie feels like she's
going crazy. They were there just a minute ago. There were
trees there. They were there when Jackie put that first rock
through the window.

Jackie pounded on her door and Mrs. Hubert said, "It opens up the backyard, don't you think?" And now the trees are all just gone. There are holes in the backyard. There are no trees.

"Where did the trees go?" Jackie yells at her, but Mrs. Hubert's talking on the phone. She doesn't hear. She just keeps repeating herself: police, police, police. In the backyard, Jackie looks around. The branches of the first-kiss tree are gone. They were right there. Is she nuts? The holes look collapsed. This makes no sense.

Jackie meant to leave before the police arrive, but they're early. The police car pulls into the driveway.

"That's embarrassing," Jackie says when the two cops climb out of their cruiser. "You both wore the same outfit again today."

39

"Is this my one phone call?" Jackie says to the cop. "Like on TV, right?" Nobody's listening. They're all rushing in and out of the room, or talking into their telephones. Something keeps beeping in the room. "What's happening?" Jackie says. "What's going on?"

"Something about trees," the cop tells her. "We don't know what."

Jackie gets her one phone call in a small room with a few desks and more police on their phones. They all have their hands on their foreheads, and their brows are furrowed. The man next to Jackie is chewing his stapler.

"It isn't terrorists," frowning cop #1 says into the phone. "There's no reason to believe that it's terrorists."

"No, ma'am, it isn't terrorists," frowning cop #2 says into her phone. She sighs.

The cop who led Jackie in here says, "Press nine." All of the lights are flashing on the phone. Jackie presses nine. Then she dials Ann's number. Ann answers on the first ring.

"Hello?"

"Look out your window," Jackie says. "Are there any trees in your yard?"

"I can't hang out anymore," Ann says.

her,

40

They want to take Jackie's fingerprints next. Nope.

She tells the cop that she has to go to the bathroom. She uses her little girl voice.

She still doesn't want to say her magic word.

The cop pounds on the door again, and turns the knob.

The door starts to swing inward.

"Mom," Jackie says, under her breath.

She is a computer shutting down.

Door number one, no Jackie.

Door number two, no Jackie.

Door number three . . .

While the police run around the building trying to find her, Jackie sits down on the floor next to her mother, and she rubs her back through the gown. Jackie's mother doesn't look up from the toilet.

I

41

In her bedroom the map of her trees takes up half of the wall. There are green pins stuck into the map, one for each of the trees. Jackie finds the pin for 10 Osborne Street and pulls it out. She drops the green pin back in the box and fishes out a black one. It's the first black pin on the map.

She reaches up and pulls out another of the green pins, the broken-arm tree. She pushes a black pin into the map in its place.

She replaces each and every green pin with a black pin.

Ann is over to do homework.

At Jackie's building, they race up the stairs together to the apartment. Jackie's father says it's okay, so Ann calls her mom to see if she can stay over. Ann's mother has red hair and she says, "Oh of course, darling."

In bed the two girls look up at the ceiling and Ann tells Jackie that a boy called her and asked her to a movie. She sounds excited, and Jackie sits up and smiles.

"That's great!" she says. They hug, and Jackie doesn't let go. She puts her hand on Ann's shoulder and she kisses her. She puts her mouth on Ann's and Ann kisses back.

"Let's spend the night up on the roof," Ann says. There is a bit of blood on her chin from their kiss. "We can launch paper airplanes out into the street. There are no more trees. All of this paper has got to be worth a fortune," she says. "It'll be like burning hundred dollar bills."

While she folds paper airplanes with sheets from her notebook, Jackie sits on the bed. Ann is so careful, making every fold perfect. Jackie loves the way she bites her lip to concentrate. She wonders if Ann makes that face when she's getting dressed.

"I love you," Jackie says, and Ann laughs happily.

"We have these old newspapers, too," Ann says. "We could make a piñata." The shirt she's wearing is tight, and you can see the shape of her breasts, the shape of her stomach, the small curve of her back. Jackie reaches out a hand to touch Ann's stomach under her shirt, and Ann smiles and goes right back to what she's doing.

Outside on the roof, they can taste smoke and fire in the air. The neighbors are standing on their rooftops, too, looking up. The whole city is up on the rooftops. In the sky, there's some sort of eclipse happening. Ann is shielding her eyes and smiling. The two girls lay out blankets and pillows on the roof and they drink tall glasses of ice water. Ms. Garcia is there. She's on her back in a bikini, and she keeps looking over and smiling at Jackie. Ann doesn't notice.

"Don't worry yourself about it," she tells Jackie. "We've all got to go sometime."

"Should we be doing everything we ever wanted?" Jackie says.

"Sure, if you think it'll do any good," Ms. Garcia says.

She rolls over onto her front and undoes her bikini top. The roller coaster rides down bright, white hallways. Walruses crowd around Jackie.

"Have you ever seen anything like that?" Ann says, pointing up.

"It's not an eclipse," someone on the next roof is yelling. "The radio says it's some sort of meteor." But Jackie rolls her eyes. Whatever. The radio thinks everything is a meteor. It's as bad as the TV. But she has this feeling in the pit of her stomach, like the world is giving way beneath them.

"I think this is it," Ann says. "I think this is the end of the world."

"Oh," Jackie says. "I wish we had longer."

"That kiss wasn't so bad," Ann says.

But there is no meteor. Everyone is looking up, like there is, but Jackie can feel eyes behind her. There is something behind the door of the stairwell onto the roof. Everyone is staring up at the sky, but there's something behind the door. Jackie can't open it. She can see the blue light around the edges but she knows it is not her mother.

43

Jackie reaches into the suv and pulls the seat belt down around the passenger seat rock.

"I'm calling the police!" Mrs. Hubert is shrieking. There are no trees. The ground is torn up, and there are holes everywhere. Jackie looks up in the sky for a meteor, but there's nothing.

Jackie meant to leave before the police arrive.

They're early.

She makes a joke. They handcuff her. Mrs. Hubert looks genuinely concerned.

They all ride downtown.

Etc.

alive.

The roller coaster creaks under their weight while it pulls them slowly up. There's a chain underneath. You can hear it clicking. *Click click click.* Jackie would feel better if they had built this structure out of metal. The wood is creaking all around them. People are seriously injured on these things every year, but they keep them running anyway.

"If we die," Jackie says to Ms. Garcia, "they'll probably close down for a week. Tops."

"What do you care?" Ms. Garcia says. "You'll be dirt." But she smiles at Jackie with her quiet smile. Her hair is moving calmly in the wind up here. Jackie doesn't know how she can be so calm. Down below you can hear the attendants laughing about something. Jackie can still smell their cigarette smoke. They don't care what happens.

"I am going to torment and ravage these people so hard," Jackie says.

"Of course you will, dear," Ms. Garcia says. She pats Jackie on the arm, then her hand stays there.

This high up, they can see the closed sections of the fair. They can see the water, and the aquarium. There's a moment, right as they roll over the top, where Jackie feels free.

45

Ann and Jackie take the streetcar together.

They hold hands. Jackie pulls her friend close and licks her own lips just before they kiss. Ann doesn't kiss her back. Jackie pulls her tighter. She can't understand why Ann won't kiss her back. This feels right. It feels correct. Ann's arms are so hairy today.

A man and his dog are standing beside them, looking out the streetcar window. The dog smells familiar. Do all dogs smell the same? Like the ocean? It is growling at Ann.

"Huh," the man says. "There's a meteor out there." Jackie looks out the window, too, up past telephone wires and buildings, but she doesn't see it.

"What if someone catches us?" Ann says, as Jackie kisses her neck. Ann's skin is warm, and Jackie feels like she is going to come apart. She feels dizzy. The streetcar pulls to a stop. It can't stop here. There is something just outside the doors.

"I think this is happening again and again," Jackie tells Ann. Ann is crouched down looking at the dog. She growls.

The doors open. They die.

46

The woman in the house is screaming at Jackie. Jackie sighs. Yeah, yeah, yeah. She puts the rock down and leaves before the police arrive. Mrs. Hubert is left standing by her window with the phone in her hand.

Jackie rides the streetcar, but she can't keep still. Her leg bounces. Her teeth chatter. She thinks about the way she'll touch Ann, the way Ann will touch her in return. She thinks about the smooth warmth of Ann's skin. She thinks about Ann's skin under her fingers, her fingers on Ann's lips. The streetcar stops right at Ann's house. These feel like memories already.

Ann opens the door. She's dressed in blue, and Jackie throws herself on her.

"Jackie?" Ann says.

Jackie kisses her surprised lips. The room darkens. Something. Oh god. In the door behind them. Something she let inside. Glass shatters.

They die.

had

They push through the front doors of the department store, and the doorman smiles. He's standing beside a crazy guy in a lab coat. A mad scientist with ash and soot all down his coat. They call the elevator for Jackie and Ann. When the doors open, the insides are all lightning and glass vials piled on the floor. It looks like the storage locker from an old horror movie. The two girls climb in and ride up toward the ladies' gloves section, up on the roof.

"Thanks for not trying to talk me out of this," Jackie says.

"At least we're in a hospital," Ann says. She laughs.

There's a young woman working with the ladies' gloves. She smiles when she sees Jackie. Her uniform is open, and underneath you can see the smooth skin of her breasts. You can see the black marker lines, where the doctors will cut to get at the cancer. Her nametag says Patricia.

Ann moves closer to the glass display case to distract the woman. Here's the plan: Ann stands near the case, blocking the woman's view of things; Jackie trips and falls into the case. She slams her hand down as hard as she can on the glass, breaking through. And, in case that doesn't cut her up enough, she grinds her hand on the shards that fall into the case itself. They want blood. You need blood for magic.

So Ann moves in front of the sales lady. Jackie steps

forward, pretends to trip, and slams her fist into the glass. It doesn't break, though. Pain shoots up her arm, and before she can think about what she's doing, Jackie slams her fist into the case again. Again and again.

She's pounding on the case as hard as she can with her fist. Patricia is just watching calmly. Then Ann has her arms around Jackie from behind, pulling her away from the case that won't break. The woman behind the counter has taken her uniform off entirely now. She is Jackie's mother.

"Doesn't that hurt?" Jackie's mother says.

Jackie looks down at her hand, purple and swollen.

It hurts.

48

The two girls find payphones in the subway station underground. Ann has a notebook that they use, and Jackie dials with her good hand. The other hand is useless — swollen and broken and purple.

"Busy signal," Jackie says, and Ann writes it down in the notebook.

"Nine nine nine seven," Ann says, and she smiles. Jackie dials the number and listens as it rings and rings. A man answers.

"Hello," Jackie says. "Have you got Prince Albert in a can?" She can hardly get the words out, she's laughing so hard. He hangs up, and Jackie tells Ann, "Another credit agency." People are bustling past. The air down here echoes with the sounds of trains and voices. Kids yelling. A man playing the saxophone. A group of walruses beached on the very edge of the subway platform, pink and barking.

Jackie dials another number. She hears her mother's voice.

"You won't be alone, Jackie. I'll be everywhere. In every building. In every tree."

"Hey officer!" Jackie yells. "Eat it!"

They burst against his face. They burst on his shoulder and his arms. The water burns him like acid.

"Did you see the look on his face?" Ann says. "I love you."

They find him again. Ann loves Jackie.

"Eat it again, please!" Jackie yells.

He yells back. "I'm so surprised and happy in my life now!"

been

50

"Where are the trees!" Mrs. Hubert shrieks at Jackie from her window. But her voice trails off. She's looking up. "Jesus," she says. Jackie looks up, too. Still no meteor. Inside the car, Ann has the seat reclined all the way back. She has her shirt pulled up. Small perfect breasts.

"Hurry," she says. "Climb inside. We have time for one more kiss."

That's enough. No use worrying about the trees now. And whatever horror is outside the door can wait.

God. Look at her.

It hurts, when Jackie wakes up. She reaches out for Ann's hand, and Ann squeezes. That hurts, too. Jackie's hand is still bruised. She's in a hospital room. The drapes are closed, and the only light is coming from a lamp.

"How long was I unconscious?" she asks Ann. But it isn't Ann, it's a nurse. "Where's Ann? Where's my father?" Jackie's head is a confused jumble of glass and blue lights and Ann. The nurse looks tired.

"The car broke your leg, and fractured your skull," she says. "You have a concussion, and you're probably going to need to walk with a cane." She just spits it out, the way Jackie's mother did when she said she was going to die.

"I'm going to die, Jackie."

The car broke Jackie's leg. She remembers her mother standing on the sidewalk looking stunned. It wasn't her mother. Jackie is confused. It was the old lady from the department store. The stranger. The nurse checks a chart. She tells Jackie, "The car broke your leg, dear, and it fractured your skull. You have a concussion, and you're probably going to need a cane to walk." She already said that.

"Can I have some more painkillers?" Jackie says. She's not sure where the pain is coming from. It feels like it is everywhere. The nurse gives her a small paper cup, like the ones for ketchup in fast food restaurants.

Later, a doctor comes in and smiles.

"Good evening," he says. "Would you prefer if we spoke privately?"

There's nobody else here. Where is Jackie's dad?

"No," she says.

"Good. Well, I'm afraid I have bad news," the doctor tells her. His voice is so relaxing. He's calm and quiet. "You have a very small fracture right here on your skull." He points. "You have a concussion. The impact broke your leg. You're probably going to need a cane to walk. At least for a while." Jackie loves this hospital. She loves the way these pills are making her feel. Do they have someone else ready to visit her? Maybe an orderly could come in. Jackie needs to know! Did the car break her leg? Is it possible that she might need a cane to walk? Has she somehow injured her head?

"My father," Jackie asks.

The doctor looks from Jackie to her dad, who is standing beside the bed. Who has been there the whole time.

part 4

Everyone gets their happy ending

better

Martha Richards sits on the edge of the bed, with the photograph of her daughter in her hands. They haven't come in a long time, Charles and his dog. The first day without them was the hardest. She waited all afternoon for them to come. She was too nervous to eat. She even forgot her afternoon pill.

Her daughter Elizabeth was so beautiful. But the fair ride had malfunctioned, lifting her daughter just slightly too high. A head's length too high. The policeman had told her only what she needed to know. Her daughter was dead. A freak accident.

She shouldn't have let Elizabeth go. She shouldn't have let her go out that day. It was just so nice to have the house to herself for an afternoon. Martha Richards understands that there was no way she could have known. Counselors have told her that. Her husband told her. But Elizabeth is gone. And if she hadn't let her go to the fair that day, her daughter would still be here.

Now, decades later, there was Charlie, showing up every day. And Elizabeth was trying to let Martha know that there was another world after this one. They would be together again some day. That had to be it. It was her daughter. It had to be. Elizabeth.

Every day, when Charlie came knocking, Martha had wanted to cry and to fall to her knees, because she was scared. She was afraid that he was lying. She was afraid that this was some kind of trick. That he knew, somehow, what had happened, and he was tormenting her.

And worse, what if it wasn't a trick? What if her daughter really was there, in the hallway every day, and Martha admitted that she believed him, and then the message was delivered? What if that was all, and Charlie stopped seeing her spirit? Her daughter would go away, having delivered her message, and Martha would be alone again.

There was only one way she could deal with it. She had to pretend she didn't believe. Pretend she didn't understand. And every day Charlie would come back with his dog, standing on the left side of the door, always careful to leave space for her invisible daughter. Elizabeth. And Martha could almost feel her there. She could. That was as close to having her daughter back as she'd ever been.

But Charlie and his dog hadn't come for a month now.

53

When Charlie opens his eyes at three a.m. the soundless mouth is right there, inches from his own face, the lips moving, the eyes staring. Charlie shoves himself back against the wall, and reaches out for Mitchie at the foot of the bed, but Mitchie isn't there. Mitchie's gone. Charlie is alone with that headless thing.

You don't get used to a headless monstrosity.

"What do you want?" Charlie says, and the thing moves its lips uselessly.

So Charlie calls Julia, sitting with his chair facing the corner, so he doesn't have to look at that face, opening and closing its mouth like a fish. But Julia is no help, either.

"She needs you, Dad," Julia says. "She has unfinished business in this world."

"What is the matter with you?" Charlie asks his daughter. "Any sane person would have told me to go to the doctor. I'm seeing a headless apparition every day. Maybe my medications are conflicting. You should see the list of side effects on this stuff."

"Headless ghosts?" Julia says. "Is that a side effect?"

"My sole companion is gone," Charlie says. "My best friend. And now I'm seeing the apparition more often? You don't think those two things are connected? You don't think maybe I've started to lose my grip? Maybe I need even more medication. Maybe I need help."

"No, she's the one who needs help, Dad. She needs someone to speak for her. She needs revenge."

"I wish Mitchie were here," Charlie says. "Mitchie didn't take any shit off this ghost."

54

After his phone conversation, Charlie tries to get back to sleep, but he can't. When he closes his eyes, she's there, trickling blood onto the floor. When he opens his eyes and turns on all the lights, she's still there.

Charlie locks himself in the bathroom, setting out a blanket and pillow on the floor, but when he turns back around to sit, there she is, standing in the shower. Bloodied and headless. Just waiting. Is the rest of his life going to be like this? He can't handle that.

"Just leave me alone," Charlie says. "Find someone else to watch you go and point at that old woman." But she stays. She stands there bleeding and moving her lips. And so Charlie lifts the heavy lid off the toilet tank, and he lets it fall to the floor. It cracks in two, and the sound is loud and violent in the bathroom. The ghost just stands there, watching.

Charlie goes to the kitchen and takes a long thin knife from the drawer.

"Fine," he says. "You want revenge? I can help you get revenge. Is that what you want? Can you even hear me?"

The ghost's face is expressionless. The knife feels wrong in Charlie's hand. But everything is wrong. He imagines Mitchie out in the cold night, wandering blind in the woods, looking for Charlie's warm arm to snuggle underneath. There's no way he would have lasted on his own. So helpless and stupid.

"I'll help you get her," Charlie says to the ghost. Oh god, could the ghost hear the uncertainty in his voice? What does he think he's going to do, wave the knife at her? "I'll help you," Charlie says, "but you have to help me too, okay? You have to help me find my friend Mitchie."

55

The walls here are so far apart. Jackie is a ghost ship in the fog. The loudest sound she makes is when she pushes the elevator button. *Click.* Even the elevator walls are far apart.

Her father is nervous. She should be in bed.

"This is the only tree I never visited," Jackie is telling him. He knows about the map now, about the broken-arm tree, the first-kiss tree. He wasn't there when Jackie broke her arm. He was long gone when she had her first kiss. Jackie tells him about Ann and Ms. Garcia. She tells him about Mrs. Hubert and about smashing her car windows because she cut down that tree. He knows about Jackie's magic word.

"Oh, chickadee," he said. But nothing else.

They find the signs to the oncology wing. They follow the big pink dots on the floor and walls. Jackie's mother's tree is in one of these lobbies. It sounds like someone is whispering, but when she looks around, the sound stops. One of her crutches slides out from under her, but her father is there, and Jackie regains her balance.

The tree is not where she remembers it was. It's been too long. Jackie looks around. This feels like the place. But there's no tree. Her father's arm around her is warm.

The nurse is on the phone.

"Where's my tree?" Jackie demands. The nurse just

keeps talking. Jackie lifts her crutch over her head and slams it down on the nurse's station. Everything in the room stops. "Where is my dead-mom tree?" she says. The nurse looks up calmly.

"Hold, please," she says into the phone. She pushes a button and sets the phone down. She looks at Jackie. Jackie can't keep her balance without the crutch.

"There was a tree here," Jackie says. The nurse looks annoyed at first, but then she looks worried. She reaches out to touch Jackie's arm across the counter.

"Are you supposed to be wandering around?" she says. "What's your name, honey?" She looks at Jackie's father, and Jackie can see the disapproval. He should never have let his daughter wander like this.

"I am a patient," Jackie tells her, "and there was a tree here in this lobby. Right there." Jackie points to the empty spot beside the bench. She feels weird. The crutch seems to be sliding to the side, slipping out from under her.

The nurse shrugs her shoulders. "We got rid of those when we redecorated," she says. "Years ago."

"What do you mean, got rid of them?" But now the nurse is picking up the phone. Jackie is chewing the inside of her cheek, trying to stay calm. Anger doesn't solve anything. Jackie's father puts his hand on her shoulder from behind.

"I'm going to call someone to help you back to your room," the nurse says. And Jackie lurches forward and wraps her arms around the old computer monitor on the nurse's station. She can't stand properly. She wants to rip this screen off her desk and smash it on the floor. But she can't lift it.

All her arm hair is standing up. Her mouth tastes like blood. But she can't do it. Then her father is there, putting his arms around the computer monitor too, and they are lifting it together.

He is lifting it up with her, even though Jackie knows that he is worried. She knows that they will have to buy a new monitor. She knows that when this is over, she is going to have to talk to somebody, too. She is crazy. She is too violent. Anger never solves anything. She hasn't let go of her mother's death. She hallucinates ghosts! She is crazy. How could her father not be worried? But right now he is helping Jackie, and they are lifting this monitor up over their heads. They lift it up over their heads, and Jackie's muscles ache like gold. The sun is shining.

"Are you insane?" the nurse says. But even crazy people can be heroes.

Smash!

daughter.

Charlie takes the elevator down with the ghost standing beside him. She makes the whole elevator cold. Even when she's not looking at him, when she's staring forward at the elevator doors, her black lips move silently, like she's given up on communicating and has simply gone mad in death.

The knife is cold in his hand. Charlie just keeps seeing Mitchie. Mitchie stuck in the corner. Mitchie trotting out of the woods, smiling. Mitchie flopping over on his side. The ghost will help him find Mitchie. This is something he has to do.

He knocks on the door of room 135, but nobody answers. Inside, Martha Richards is probably sleeping. It's the middle of the night. Charlie knocks again. The ghost waits patiently.

After the third knock, it occurs to Charlie that he can just go in. He's here to wave a kitchen knife in her face. He doesn't need to politely wait for an answer. He can just go right in.

So he pushes the door open, and a cold gust of air comes out to meet him. A different kind of cold than the ghost makes. This was a natural cold, and Charlie can see glass all over the carpet by the window. It's been smashed in. The curtains are lifting slightly in the cold wind. Mrs. Richards is on the floor, already dead. Her face is pale in the light from the window. There are shapes crowded around her. Maybe people, maybe not. There's black hair everywhere. They look like animals.

Charlie turns the light on, and a creature comes at him. It looks like a girl, but her face is all wrong. The eyes are young, but the mouth has too many teeth. They're moving around in her mouth, sliding and grinding against one another. They grind against one another and crack and split, leaving shards and jagged edges, and the girl's mouth is still opening wider. Charlie drops the knife. This is not right. The teeth sink into his shoulder. The pain is warm.

"So this is how it happens," Charlie says. Then there is a warm mouth on his neck. There's a woman above him, much bigger than the girl. She pushes the girl aside with her face, like an animal might, and she leans down, mouth open, to take a chunk out of Charlie's throat. The cold is inside him now.

Charlie looks up, and the ghost is standing there, holding its own head to watch while the creatures go about their business, pulling him apart.

The two younger creatures go back to eating Mrs. Richards. But most of Charlie ends up inside the mother. He can feel parts of his body coming away, but it doesn't hurt anymore. The mother tears strips off of him, pulling along the grain where the flesh can separate. The headless ghost's face is still expressionless, but Charlie is closer to death than life, and he can hear her voice now.

"Tell her I'm okay," the ghost says, pointing to where the two younger creatures are fighting over Mrs. Richards' body. "Tell her I'm okay. Tell her I'm okay."

The ghost can hear Charlie now, too. She listens to him moan and cry, and then, finally, when she thinks he is beyond making any more sounds, she hears his voice from inside the largest creature. The mother. From inside the bloody thing, she hears Charlie say, "Jesus, Mitchie. There you are. Do you know how worried I was?"

About the Author

Joey Comeau writes the comic *A Softer World*, which has appeared in *The Guardian* and has been profiled in *Rolling Stone*, and which *Publishers Weekly* called "subtle and dramatic." The website (asofterworld.com) has been online since 2003 and has an average daily readership of 70,000 people worldwide. His previous books include the self-published first novel, *Lockpick Pornography*, which sold out its print run of 1,000 books in just three months; *It's Too Late to Say I'm Sorry* (2007), a collection of short stories; and *Overqualified* (ECW, 2009), now in its fourth printing. Comeau lives in Toronto, Ontario.